"You're such a love," Whitney murmured.

"How come someone so sweet can have such a bad-tempered man for a father?"

Troy chuckled, as if he could understand her.

"Your papa," she continued, "is rude, arrogant...and when he was a teenager he had every girl in the valley chasing after him—except me! Luke Brannigan is a heartbreaker of the worst kind. You think I'm being too hard on him? Well, tell you what, if I can ever *find* something good to say about him, you'll be the first to know. But don't hold your breath!"

Dear Reader

A special delivery! We are proud to announce our bouncing baby series! Each month we'll be bringing you your very own bundle of joy—a cuddly and delightful romance by one of your favourite authors. This series is all about the true labour of love—parenthood and how to survive it! Because, as our heroes and heroines are about to discover, two's company and three (or four...or five) is a family!

And next month's arrival will be:

Found: One Father
by
Shannon Waverly

When Jill became pregnant accidentally with baby Maddy she thought that Aidan's insistence that he never wanted children would disappear once the child was born—but it didn't. Until he was involved in a fateful plane crash resulting in amnesia, and suddenly the perfect father emerged!

Happy reading!

The Editors

Grace Green was born in Scotland and is a former teacher. In 1967 she and her marine engineer husband John emigrated to Canada where they raised their four children. Empty-nesters now, they are happily settled in West Vancouver in a house overlooking the ocean. Grace enjoys walking the sea wall, gardening, getting together with other writers...and watching her characters come to life, because she knows that, once they do, they will take over and write her stories for her.

BRANNIGAN'S BABY

BY

GRACE GREEN

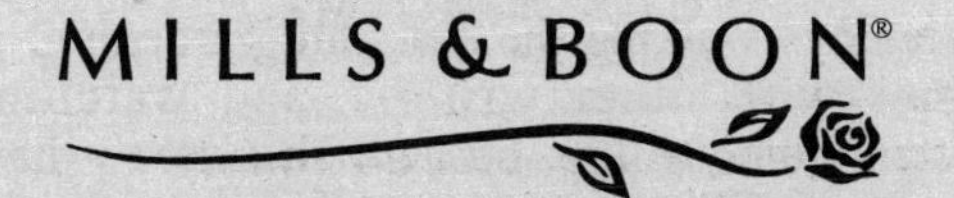

FOR MIKE HANNAY

First published in Great Britain 1997
Harlequin Mills & Boon Limited,
Eton House, 18-24 Paradise Road, Richmond, Surrey TW9 1SR

ISBN 0 263 80231 0

Set in Times Roman 11 on 12 pt.
02-9708-44680 C1

Printed and bound in Great Britain
by Mackays of Chatham PLC, Chatham

CHAPTER ONE

WHEN WORD GOT AROUND that Luke Brannigan was back in town, business at Hetty's Beauty Salon picked up within the hour.

'Dixie Mae saw him get off the Greyhound bus, didn't you, Dix?' Beth Armour wriggled excitedly in her seat as Hetty worked styling mousse into her hair.

'Sure did.' Seated next to her, Dixie kept her eyes fixed admiringly on her own reflection in the mirror. ''Course, I just saw him from the distance, but that sexy swagger...'

She shrugged. *Unmistakable.*

'Where was he going then?' somebody asked. 'Home?'

'Looked that way. He hiked off along the side road that winds up through the vineyards to Brannigan House.'

'He must've heard his grandmother passed away.' Patsy Smith's voice came from under one of the dryers. 'But if he got off that bus, he'd be too late for the funeral. He'll be rich now,' she went on dreamily. 'And he'll have every female in the valley chasin' after him, just like before—'

'*Every female 'cept for Whitney McKenzie.*'

Dixie's declaration was met with a moment of silence.

Then Beth said, quietly, 'That's right. There was

no love lost between those two. And now he's back, he'll send her packing! Well, you can't blame him, considering…'

Patsy sighed. 'Cressida Brannigan made one huge mistake taking that girl into her home. Hadn't been for her, Luke woulda *never* gone and taken off the way he did. He and his gran were close…*real* close… before…'

Begonia Bright poked her head out from under the end dryer. 'I'd give most anything—' her beady eyes glittered '—to be a fly on the wall when *those* two meet again.'

And though none of the others really liked Begonia, they all, without exception, felt exactly the same way.

Whitney McKenzie eased her aching feet out of her high-heeled black pumps and shifted wearily in the leather wing chair. Cressida's funeral had been emotionally draining, as had been the long year leading up to it. She needed time alone, peace to start grieving…

And a chance to catch up on lost sleep.

Swallowing back an incipient yawn, she tried to look alert as Edmund Maxwell—senior partner of Maxwell and Maxwell, the only law firm in the nearby Okanagan town of Emerald, B.C.—extricated a document from his briefcase. He set the case on top of Cressida's intricately carved Chinese desk, and moved his stooped figure across to the hearth.

Somberly his gaze passed over the trio seated before him in the Brannigan House library: Whitney, Alice the cook and Myrna the housemaid.

'It is no longer the custom,' he began, 'for lawyers to read out wills; however, as I'm sure you all know, the late Cressida Brannigan cared not one jot for custom. So, in accordance with her declared wishes, I shall now read out to you her Last Will and—'

The door behind Whitney clicked open.

Edmund Maxwell lifted his head, and over the top of his half glasses frowned at the intruder.

Slumping back in her seat, Whitney closed her eyes. She felt exhaustion seep into her very bones—

'*What the hell's going on here*?' A male voice, aggressive and vaguely familiar, rasped into the quiet room.

Whitney's eyes flew open.

'*And where the devil*,' the voice challenged as it continued, '*is my grandmother*?'

Whitney shot bolt upright. *Grandmother*?

Aghast, she peered around the wing of her armchair—and when she saw the man standing in the doorway, her heart slammed against her ribs with such force it knocked every particle of breath from her lungs.

He was back.

Luke was back.

Her shocked gaze darted over him jerkily, snapping him, in a series of flashes, like a camera...

The straw blond hair that curled to his collar—snap!

The lean, tanned face, with its high-slashed cheekbones, electric blue eyes and thin sensual lips—snap!

The wide shoulders—snap!

The narrow hips—snap!

The long, powerful legs—snap!

At seventeen, Luke had been tall; now he was well over six feet, but the cockiness that had been his trademark as a teenager had been replaced by something more dangerous—

'Lucas!' The lawyer's voice wobbled. 'Oh, dear. I tried to contact you—I wanted to let you know—'

'Let me know *what*?'

Something *infinitely* more dangerous. Whitney winced as she saw the steely menace in his eyes. Maturity had brought hard arrogance to the man and an aura of intensity that crackled. He'd have turned heads anywhere. Not that he was any advertisement for *GQ*—he most definitely was not! His jaw was stubbled, his shirt sweatstained, his blue jeans ragged, and worn almost white at the knees. But still—

A flash of movement over one of his shoulders caught her attention. Her gaze sliced up...and her mind reeled.

A baby?

He'd brought home a *baby*?

Oh, yes—she fought to retain her grip on reality—Luke Brannigan had indeed brought home a baby.

She could see a small fisted hand waving ferociously over Luke's shoulder—the infant must be in some kind of a backpack; she could also now see a blue hat, rakishly askew, and beneath its floppy brim part of a small face.

'I said—' Luke's tone was grim '—let me know *what*?'

He still hadn't noticed her; hadn't for a second removed his searing gaze from the lawyer. She swiveled around to stare at Edmund Maxwell, waiting for his reply...

Only to be met with a look of mute appeal...and a pointed nod in her direction. Dismayed, she pressed a fist to her breast. *Me*? she mouthed back.

He nodded.

Whitney swallowed. She wanted to shrink back in her seat; wanted never to have Luke Brannigan's eyes find her...

But there was no way out; she was, after all, in charge here—at least until after the reading of the will, when the new owner of the estate was named. Which would, of course, be Luke. He was a Brannigan and—as far as Cressida had been aware—the last of the line; so, despite their estrangement, she'd never have left the estate to anyone but him.

Whitney wriggled her feet back into her pumps, dragged her palms down her black linen skirt and stood up.

She turned to face her old enemy. His eyes had never looked bluer; against his tan, they dazzled like sapphires. Sapphires that had been dipped in ice water.

He blinked. Looked at her blankly. And blinked again.

Whitney knew the exact second he recognized her...and knew, by the sneer that swiftly curled his upper lip, that nothing had changed.

Between *them*, nothing had changed.

She took in a deep breath.

'Your grandmother,' she said, 'died three days ago. The funeral was earlier this afternoon. And now Mr.

Maxwell is going to read Cressida's will, so if you'll find yourself a seat, we can continue—'

'Dead?' Luke's face had paled. 'You mean, I'm too late to—'

'Yes, yes.' The papers in Edmund Maxwell's hands shook. 'Yes, too late, I'm afraid. And now…the will. If we are all ready, shall we get on with it?'

Luke seemed too stunned to answer.

Whitney nodded and sat down. She twined her fingers together in her lap, and desperately tried to ignore the man behind her, and focus her attention on Edmund Maxwell.

The lawyer began by reading out details of bequests to Cook and Myrna, both in their early seventies. Then he read out a list of smaller bequests—to several old friends; to her church; to the Emerald Valley Elementary School.

'And to Whitney McKenzie—'

Whitney swallowed to relieve the aching lump that had risen in her throat. Whatever bequest she received would never make up for the loss of this woman she'd loved so dearly. She blinked back threatening tears…

'—to my beloved Whitney, I leave Brannigan House, the Emerald Valley Vineyards and the remainder of my estate.'

Her mind went blank…other than one single question that rocketed about, back and forth, in her brain, making her dizzier and dizzier by the moment: *Why not Luke*?

The lawyer continued to talk, but she assimilated nothing. Her mind was in overload, unable to cope with the enormity of what had just happened—

'Miss McKenzie?'

She came to with a jump, and realized Edmund Maxwell must have finished. He was standing leaning over her.

'My dear,' he said, 'if you would see me to the door, I should like to talk with you…privately…before I leave.'

Somehow Whitney managed to rouse herself, even managed a weak smile as the staff murmured words of congratulation. Distantly she was aware Luke was no longer in the room. Had he taken off, as soon as he'd discovered there was nothing for him here? Oh, God, she prayed, let it be so.

She said her final goodbyes to Cook and Myrna, who had a taxi waiting and were about to leave Brannigan House for good. Once they had departed, Whitney escorted the lawyer through the front hall and out to the heavy oak door.

He stood on the stoop, his frail body bowed, his coat collar turned up against the brisk spring breeze.

'It's a burden,' he said, 'and of course Cressida herself was to blame. She's kept the house up these past years, but as for the vineyards…well, she didn't move with the times. There was little money coming in latterly, and I'm afraid she used up all her capital. Her death, to be blunt, was timely. After honoring the bequests she specified, there won't be one red cent left in her account.'

'I had no idea.' Whitney shivered as the wind cut through her black silk blouse. 'She was always so lackadaisical about money…I assumed she had plenty of it!'

'At one time she did.' He tucked his briefcase under his arm while he pulled on a pair of worn black leather gloves. 'You must think over your options very carefully, my dear. Best to sell, but Lucas's turning up right now…well, that *is* a complication. You'll have to talk things over with him. And let me know what you decide.'

'Yes,' she murmured, 'of course.'

But even as she spoke, relief trembled through her. Edmund Maxwell had obviously not noticed that his own car was the only vehicle left in the forecourt. He'd been wrong in thinking Luke's arrival presented a complication.

The man—thank the Lord!—had already gone.

The funeral reception had been held in the drawing room.

Whitney had replenished the fire there earlier, before going with the lawyer and the servants to the library. Now, lost in her troubled thoughts, she made her way back there. She closed the door behind her, and with a sigh, crossed to the hearth, seeking warmth and comfort from the flames.

With her arms clasped around her waist, she stared down unhappily into the leaping orange and yellow tongues.

'Oh, Cressida,' she murmured, 'what have you done?'

'What indeed!' drawled a cynical voice from behind.

Feeling as if her body had jumped clean out of its skin, she swirled around with a loud gasp.

Luke Brannigan was getting up from a high-backed sofa, where he'd deposited his sleeping child. Tilted against the sofa was a huge, dirty-white canvas duffel bag, a jarring note, she decided abstractedly, in this elegant room.

He walked toward her, his tall frame moving between her and the doorway, blocking her means of escape—

Now why should she think she might need to escape? Oh, she knew why! His bold gaze was roaming over her with blatant male appreciation...lingeringly...as if he just couldn't *wait* to get his hands where his eyes already were.

She stiffened.

'Yes, what indeed,' he repeated, and this time his tone was mocking. 'But thank the Lord for codicils.'

'What on *earth* are you talking about?'

His brows tugged together, as if she'd taken him aback...and then he gave a short derisive laugh.

'You didn't hear, did you! You were so wrapped up in delight at your own good fortune that you didn't bother listening as Maxwell read out the finer points of the will.'

'The *finer* points.'

'The codicil. I guess Cressida still had a soft spot for me, despite our long estrangement—'

'This codicil...' Whitney's cool tone revealed nothing of her rising sense of alarm. 'What did it say?'

'Pour me a drink and I'll tell you.'

Whitney hesitated, briefly, and then with her lips compressed into a thin line, she crossed to the small buffet that served as a liquor cabinet.

'What'll you have?' she asked curtly.

'Scotch. Neat.'

She poured his drink but as she made to lift the glass, he said, 'Are you going to make me drink alone?'

A drink might help steady her nerves, which were prickling; warning her of some danger ahead. She poured herself a rye, added a splash of ginger ale.

She placed his glass on the mantelpiece, and walked to the window. Then turned, so her back was to the light.

'So.' She took a sip of her drink, felt the fire of it race through her blood. 'Tell me—'

'Know something? I didn't recognize you at first. The last time I saw you, you were still a scrawny twelve-year-old, with legs like twigs and pigtails the color of new carrots. But now—'

'Yes?' Whitney tilted her chin. She knew perfectly well what she looked like now, but it would be some sort of small revenge to have him admit how she'd changed.

How she'd...improved.

'You're a knockout,' he said softly. 'Even in that drab black outfit, you're a knockout. Your figure, those green eyes and creamy skin, that fantastic flame red hair—lady, you're drop-dead gorgeous...and you obviously know it. Just as you must know—' his voice had become icy '—that you are the image of your late and unlamented mother.'

Whitney felt as winded as if he'd thrown her down a flight of stairs. 'Yes.' Somehow she managed to keep her voice steady. 'I do *look* like my mother.'

'Krystal would've been proud of you.' His tone chilled her. 'You've succeeded where she failed. You now own Brannigan House and the Emerald Valley Vineyards—and unlike your beautiful mother, who broke up a marriage in her unsuccessful attempt to achieve her goal, you had it handed to you on a platter. So tell me...' He swallowed his Scotch in one gulp and rolled the empty glass between his hands. 'What bargain did you make with the Devil, in order that you might inherit this paradise on earth?'

Because of her red hair, Whitney knew people expected her to have a temper. Which she did. But usually she managed to control it...and she was certainly not about to let *this* man know he was getting under her skin!

'As you say, this house is now mine...and I'm not prepared to be *insulted* in it!' She ignored an unexpected stab of compunction. Even if Luke had more right to the estate than she, she was honor-bound to respect the terms of the will. 'I'm going up to change,' she added cuttingly, 'and when I come down, please be gone. If you're not—'

His hand on her shoulder was rough, the unexpectedness of his move making her cry out as he spun her around.

'You're forgetting one thing,' he said, with soft menace.

'*What*?'

He smiled, and when she saw the triumph in his eyes, apprehension quivered through her.

'The codicil,' he said. 'The terms of the codicil—'

'I'm sure they don't concern me!'

'Ah, but they do. Grandmother's codicil states—'

'Edmund Maxwell left a copy of the will in the library.' Whitney wrenched herself free. 'I'll read it for myself!'

The library was empty, and she hurried across to the desk. Snatching up the will, she flipped to the last page.

When she read the words typed there, she felt as if she'd stepped onto quicksand. She put a hand on the desktop to steady herself—

'So you see—' Luke had come up behind her '—I'm to be living here, at Brannigan House, with you. And as long as I want to stay here, you may never sell the estate.'

'It *says*,' Whitney struggled to contain a feeling of panic, 'that if you show up here on the day of the funeral, penniless and seeking shelter, I may not turn you away...and under those circumstances alone, I may not sell.' She fixed him with a scathing gaze. 'You're now twenty-nine—'

'Thirty.' His eyes taunted her. 'Just turned.'

'You don't expect me to believe you've come back after thirteen years with nothing but the shirt on your back—'

'Not only that,' he murmured, 'but with a nine-month-old son to support. Cressida, bless her heart, must have known that one day I'd—'

'Must have known you'd never amount to anything, Luke Brannigan!' She glared at him. 'Thank heavens your grandmother didn't live to see this day!'

'Now that's where I beg to differ,' he said mildly. 'But right now I don't have the strength to argue—

I've been on the road since yesterday and I'm beat. If you'll show me where we're to be quartered...' He moved across to the sofa, where he scooped up the baby, before easily swinging up his enormous bulging duffel bag. 'I'd like to get settled in.'

Whitney put a hand to her brow, and felt her fingers tremble. Was she really stuck with this man? Was selling the estate not an option? If that was the case, how was she going to cope! Edmund Maxwell had said that Cressida had run out of money; she, Whitney, had a couple of thousand dollars in her own bank account...but that kind of money was peanuts, compared to what would be needed to make the Emerald Valley Vineyard a profitable entity again.

'Why don't you just take over your father's suite.' With a distracted gesture, she shoved back her hair.

'I'd prefer not to use my father's rooms.' His jaw tightened. 'How about the one looking down on the pool?'

'No,' Whitney said stiffly. 'That's mine.'

'Then I'll take the one next door.' He raised his brows. 'Any problem with that?'

Yes, she wanted to say. A big problem. The last thing she wanted was to have him sleeping in the next room to hers. 'That'll be fine. For now.'

The baby shifted, muttered and snuggled his face against Luke's shirt. And Luke dropped an absent kiss on top of the child's head, on the crown of the blue hat.

Something about the picture tugged Whitney's heart; and as Luke turned on his heel and strode off, she stared after him, wondering why she felt so emotionally affected. Was it because Luke was so hard and invulnerable, while his child was trusting and helpless? Was it the tenderness of his gesture that had touched her heart? She didn't *want* to think of Luke as tender; she wanted to keep believing him to be horrid and arrogant...and impossible.

Only then would she feel justified in using every trick she could come up with in order to get rid of him. Where was the mother of his child? Was she alive? Were they married? Divorced? Had they indeed ever *been* married? Was she still in his life?

One question she didn't need to ask herself, because she already knew the answer. Luke still hated her...just as he'd hated her thirteen years before, when Cressida Brannigan had brought her to live at Brannigan House.

Looking at it now, from an adult point of view, she didn't find Luke's attitude toward her so surprising. After all, she *had* been the cause of all the quarrels between him and his grandmother, in particular that last ugly quarrel that had led to Cressida's giving Luke the ultimatum that had resulted in Luke's leaving the family home.

Whitney had always felt burdened by guilt over that, because Luke had disappeared, never to be heard from again.

Till today.

On learning of his grandmother's death, he'd appeared shocked. Had he been? Or was he just a very good actor?

It was possible that word of Maxwell's attempts to contact him *had* reached him. It was also equally possible that his arrival at Brannigan House, on this particular day, had been sheer coincidence. After all, it was a well-known fact that truth was stranger than fiction. And it didn't really matter, did it! The bottom line was that he *had* turned up, like the proverbial bad penny...

Whitney frowned. Hc'd said he had no money. If indeed he was penniless, then he was entitled to move into this house and make it his home.

But she was not about to take his claim at face value. She had a responsibility to Cressida, to make sure the terms of her will were carried out to the letter.

She'd get Edmund Maxwell onto it immediately, have him make some investigations...and ferret out the truth.

CHAPTER TWO

'WELL, I *am* impressed...'

Whitney hadn't heard Luke come into the kitchen. His voice startled her, and she took a moment to calm herself before turning around.

'Impressed? By what?'

He glanced at the stacks of clean dishes, and the dozens of crystal glasses, which Whitney had carefully handwashed and then polished with a linen tea towel till they sparkled. 'By your efforts to impress.'

She put her shoulder to him, and hefted up a pile of plates. 'Excuse me. I need to get into that cupboard.'

He stepped aside, and opened the cupboard door. 'You don't have to prove anything to me,' he said softly. 'I know exactly where you're coming from. Relax, honey...go pour yourself another drink and let the housekeeper finish up here.'

Keeping a tight rein on her anger, Whitney crossed to collect a second pile of plates. Pretending he didn't exist, she busied herself putting the rest of the dishes away. Then she started on the glasses, arranging as many as she could do on a large wooden tray, before carrying them out into the hall and across to the living room.

Resentfully she became aware that Luke was right behind her; a burr couldn't have stuck much closer.

He made no attempt to help as she set the glasses in the buffet.

'So.' His tone was dripping with sarcasm. 'Here we are, darlin'. Home alone.'

'I'm not in the mood for jokes—'

'Oh, it's no joke. Whoever would have thought, when you arrived here as a saucer-eyed orphan, that one day we'd be setting up house together.'

'We shall not be setting up house together. It seems, at present, that I have no option but to give you a room, but beyond that, you are *entirely* on your own. You can do your own cooking, and cleaning—'

'The servants'll look after me. That's what they're paid for.'

She turned on him sharply. 'Cook and Myrna will *not* be looking after you! They've already gone—and they won't be coming back. They were over retirement age and only stayed on as long as they did because they loved your grandmother.'

She turned on her heel and with the tray swinging from one hand, walked with purposeful steps back to the kitchen. There she began loading the remaining glasses onto the tray.

Once these were put away, she decided, she was going to soak in a hot bath and then have an early night. Her exhaustion had now intensified to the point where she knew that if she once sat down, she'd never get up again!

'I tried to get into the attic,' Luke's voice came from behind, making her grit her teeth, 'but it's locked. Do you have the key?'

She didn't look at him; continued to load the glasses. 'What do you want it for?'

'I remember my grandmother as being something of a pack rat, and there's a faint hope that my own nursery furniture might be still up there—I know it used to be, when I was a boy. Do you happen to—'

'It's still there…along with an old stroller. But it'll all be covered in dust. I've had no time to do any cleaning in the attic this past year, and Myrna wasn't up to climbing those steep, narrow stairs.'

'So…where's the key?'

'On the shelf above the door.' Finally she turned. 'You're not going up there tonight? Even if you did bring the cot down, you couldn't put your baby in it yet—the mattress will need to be aired, the woodwork washed down.'

He rubbed a hand against his nape, and she noticed, for the first time, that his eyes were strained, his expression weary. If he hadn't been so arrogant and hostile, she might have felt a twinge of concern…or even sympathy.

'You're right,' he said. 'In the morning, then.'

'Where will you put the baby tonight?'

'He can sleep with me.'

Lucky baby! she thought…and immediately felt a wave of shock; where had *that* thought come from! She turned abruptly and reached out for the tray, but in her haste she knocked over a crystal sherry glass. It fell to the floor, shattering on the terra-cotta tiles.

With a murmur of dismay, she crouched down, but as she scrabbled to pick up the pieces, she felt a prick of pain. She bit her lip as she saw blood beading on her finger…

A strong hand pulled her to her feet.

'Here.' Luke's voice was gruff. 'Let me see.'

He held her hand in his, squeezing the finger gently.

'No glass in there,' he murmured. 'At least, I don't think so…'

She struggled against a feeling of grogginess as he walked her over to the sink. He turned on the cold tap, and held her finger under it.

He was standing right behind her, so close she could feel the warmth of his body against her own. She could also hear him breathing. She felt the hair at her crown stir. And heard his breathing quicken.

'You smell like peaches.' His voice was low, sexy, seductive.

She wanted to move, but she was trapped between him and the sink. Besides, she doubted her shaky legs were capable of taking her anywhere. Her finger under the cold tap began to feel numb. She noticed the bleeding had stopped, and she tugged her hand free from his grasp.

He swung her around, and his eyes were dark. 'Do you *taste* like peaches?'

He held her right shoulder with his left hand, and with his other, brushed a finger lightly down her left cheek; trailed it across to the corner of her mouth; let the tip linger. 'I know you'd like me to find out.'

She wanted to jerk her face back, but his blue eyes had hypnotized her into immobility. 'You're crazy!'

'I know you're attracted to me. I could tell by the

way your pupils dilated, when we were discussing who would sleep where—and with whom...'

His words drew all the strength from her body. 'You're crazy,' she repeated, this time in a thready whisper.

'Am I?' The back of his fingernail scraped across her teeth. 'And what about you? Are you...*greedy*?' His voice had all at once become angry, bitter. 'As greedy...as your mother was?'

He'd been playing with her; testing her...

Cheeks burning with humiliation and resentment, she shoved him away from her abruptly.

He laughed, and the harsh sound grated in her ears. She wanted to press her hands to them, to blank out the sound. But she wouldn't give him that satisfaction.

'If you'll get out of here,' she said in a glacial tone, 'I'll finish up. It's been an exhausting day and I'm going to have an early night—'

'I'll clean up.'

'No, *I*'ll clean up!'

'You've already cut yourself once. You want me to have to play doctor again? You want more of that? Okay, then, go ahead.'

She couldn't win; not with this man. But she really was all in; she felt as if she would keel over, any minute now—

Impatiently, he barked, 'Well?'

'All *right*. I'll go.' She hesitated. 'But...what about...won't you...need any help with...the baby?'

'I can manage just fine, without having to resort to anyone...particularly a female...for help.'

'Well, good for you! But don't forget...I did offer.'

On her way out, she slammed the door behind her...hard.

A knockout. That's what he'd called her.

And the image of her mother.

Green eyes dark with distress, Whitney drew the bristle brush through her glossy red hair one last time, before putting the brush down on the dresser. Then rising from the padded stool, she crossed to the wardrobe and slid open the bottom drawer. From under a pile of assorted cashmere sweaters, she extricated a silver-framed photograph.

A picture of her mother...and Luke's father, Ben.

For the past thirteen years Whitney had kept it hidden. She'd taken it out only when she was alone...and had become adept at quickly tucking it away at the sound of Cressida's light tap on her door.

She'd hated acting so furtively, despite doing so with the best of intentions...and even now, even knowing Cressida was beyond being hurt, she couldn't help feeling guilty.

But there was no reason to.

She had done nothing wrong.

It was her mother who had done that. Adultery could never be excused, no matter the circumstances—

Whitney gave herself a shake and reined in her drifting thoughts. She must go to bed; she needed to get some sleep. Tomorrow, she'd have to cope with Luke.

Until Edmund Maxwell could get her the ammunition she required to get rid of her unwanted guest, she'd have to find a way to divide the house between them, so she could avoid him as much as possible. He would fight the idea, of course. He would want to have the run of the place as he had done when he was growing up. She'd better have her wits about her. He would be a crafty opponent.

Pushing herself to her feet, she crossed to the dresser and defiantly set up the framed picture.

There was no longer any need to hide it. Only one person in the world could conceivably be offended by its presence here at Brannigan House...

Luke.

And if she was sure of nothing else, she was sure of this: It would be a frosty Friday indeed before she'd ever invite *that* man into her bedroom!

'Ah, you're up.' Luke closed his bedroom door behind him just as Whitney came out of her own room the next morning. 'Do you normally lie in bed this late?'

Coffee. Whitney swept past him and made for the stairs. She always needed that first cup of coffee to get her going...but today, she needed it much more than she normally did, in order to be able to cope with this man.

'One could hardly sleep with that racket you've been making in the attic,' she said over her shoulder. 'I assume,' she added, as she ran down the stairs with his heavy tread not far behind her, 'you found what you needed?'

'Yup. Everything's washed down, and I have the cot mattress airing in front of the living room fire.'

Hand on the banister, she jolted to a stop, and looked back up at him with an eyebrow cocked ironically. 'So you're not above setting a fire and getting it going?'

'Needs must, when the devil drives.'

'Whom.'

'Whom what?'

'"He must needs go *whom* the devil doth drive."'

'So...you got yourself an education while I've been away. And who paid for that, I wonder?'

She subjected him to a rigid glance but wasn't so angry that she didn't see, before she jerked her gaze away again, that he was wearing a crisp white T-shirt and black jeans. In that one glance she'd also noticed that his hair was still damp from his shower, and that he'd shaved; the cleft on his chin was now visible—a cleft she'd forgotten was there. Thirteen years was a long time, after all...and she'd been just twelve when she'd known him before.

Known him...she smiled self-derisively as she stalked to the kitchen...now that was a misnomer. She'd never *known* him. They'd lived in the same house for a few months, that was all—the most awful months of her life. She'd just lost her mother; and she'd cowed in terror as Luke had fought savagely with his grandmother over the elderly woman's decision to give a home to this girl Luke hated so viciously.

The ongoing battle had culminated in that last dreadful row, when Luke had called her those ugly names, yelling them at her, after describing her mother and Ben Brannigan in words she'd never heard before and didn't understand.

But Cressida had heard…and she had understood.

Shaking with anger, she'd ordered Luke to apologize or get out.

He'd shouted that he was going to leave.

And she'd called after him not to come back, then, till he was ready to say he was sorry.

He'd never, apparently, been ready to do so.

And it wasn't till Whitney was almost fourteen that she realized Luke's leaving had broken his grandmother's heart.

'You ought to try to find him,' Whitney had said one day, stumblingly.

'I have my pride, child.' Cressida had replied, her slender back ramrod straight as always. 'I have my pride.'

And was it pride that had kept Luke away?

But even if she knew the answer to that, Whitney reflected, what good would it do now?

'I'm going to make coffee.' She pushed the kitchen door open and went in. 'And then we'll talk. We have things to discuss.'

He leaned back against the fridge as she poured cold water into the coffeemaker. 'Tell me,' he said, 'about my grandmother. She'd been ill for some time?'

'She fell a year ago and broke her hip. It seemed to be taking a long time to heal so the doctors ran some tests. They discovered a tumor—' Whitney cleared her throat of a sudden huskiness. 'Strong coffee okay with you?'

'Stronger the better.'

She measured eight scoops into the filter, and switched on the coffeemaker. 'She was very weak by the time they sent her home from hospital, and for the next ten months or so, she passed most of her time in bed.'

'And in pain?'

'Yes.' Understatement of the century.

'Why the hell didn't you try to contact me?'

'She didn't want me to.'

He swore vehemently.

'You had thirteen years.' Her tone was heavily laced with accusation. 'Why did you never come home?'

'She told me to leave.'

'Oh, for heaven's sake, you sound like a spoiled child! All you had to do was say you were sorry.'

'I wasn't sorry.' He pushed himself from the fridge and crossed to the sink. Grasping the countertop edge with white-knuckled hands, he stared out the uncurtained window. 'What my grandmother did—taking you in—was unforgivable.'

'Your grandmother was a warm and compassionate woman.' Whitney fought to keep control of her emotions. 'I know it must have been hard for you to understand her actions—after all, you were only seventeen and had been very badly hurt—'

'I wasn't thinking of myself!' He whirled around and his eyes reflected more than a decade of built-up pent-up resentment at her. 'I was thinking of my *mother*. Of what they—my father and your mother—had done to her—'

'Don't!' Shaking, Whitney put up her hands to stop him. 'Please don't let's start all this over again. I do understand why you're so resentful, but, Luke, for your own sanity you have to put it all behind you—'

'Don't you think I've tried? Don't you think I've tried to forgive? To forgive and forget? What do you think it did to me, walking away from my grandmother, the one person in the world who meant anything to me? And now—' he swung an arm out wildly '—to come back to this house, and find I'm too late—my God, it's ripping me apart!'

Taut silence vibrated through the kitchen following Luke's outburst, a silence suddenly broken by the wavering cry of a baby.

Whitney looked around confusedly.

Luke exhaled a heavy breath, and said wearily, 'It's the baby monitor. Over by the bread bin.'

She saw it then, a blue-and-white gadget, with a red light flickering.

'I haven't seen one of those before.' Her voice came out stiltedly, but she kept going. 'You leave one part in the baby's room, and set the other up wherever you are?'

'That's right. I'll just go up and fetch him...'

'What's his name?'

'Troy,' he said over his shoulder, as he left the room.

Troy. Short for Troilus? The names Troilus and Cressida were indelibly linked in literature; had Luke, despite his estrangement from his grandmother, remembered the elderly woman with love as he'd chosen a name for his son?

When he returned, the coffee was ready, and she'd just filled two mugs and put sugar and cream in her own.

She'd been determined to keep any communication between them on a purely impersonal and businesslike level, but she made the fatal mistake of looking at the baby in his arms.

'Why...he's dark!'

'I guess you didn't see him without his hat yesterday.' Luke ruffled his son's wispy black hair, and the child chuckled and blew out a bubble. His lashes were as dark as his hair, but he had his father's blue eyes. He was wearing a red sweatshirt, with a pair of red corduroy dungarees.

He was beautiful, adorable...and he melted her heart.

'Could you unhitch that tray,' Luke said, 'so I can get him into his seat? Those catches baffled me.'

It took Whitney a couple of moments to get the hang of them herself, but she finally managed. After Luke had seated the baby, she clicked it in place again.

'So...' She stepped back, uncomfortably aware of his closeness. 'What does he have for breakfast?'

'Today, he'll have a banana and toast, some milk...'

'I don't have any bananas '

'I've brought enough food to last him a couple of days. Then I thought,' he went on as he took a brown bag from the fridge, 'you might drive me into town and I can stock up on supplies. My credit was always good at Stanley's corner store, so I'm sure it'll—'

'Jim Stanley died years ago. His store was bulldozed, and you'll find a superstore there now. You'll have to go to the bank, if you've no money…and get a loan.'

He toppled the contents of the bag on the table: a bunch of ripe bananas, a small loaf of bread, a container of wheat germ, a pint carton of skim milk. 'To get a loan, a person needs collateral. Looks as if I'm going to be depending on you for supplies. But Troy and I don't eat much—do we, monster?' He grinned down at the baby, and the baby grinned back—showing two small white teeth—as if they were sharing some huge joke.

Whitney felt a violent surge of resentment. So…Luke thought he could stay on here, living off her own meager bank account.

No way.

He'd already peeled a banana and diced it. Now he dipped the squares in milk, rolled them in the wheat germ and began setting them on the plastic tray. Reluctantly intrigued—not only by the economy of Luke's movements but by his lean, tanned fingers with their smooth rounded nails—she wanted to stay and watch. Instead she set his coffee mug on the table along with the creamer and sugar bowl.

'I'm going through to the living room,' she said crisply, as the baby with intense concentration picked up a banana morsel. 'I have some phone calls to make—'

'You'll be calling Maxwell, I guess, and asking him to make enquiries about me. Let me save you both some time.' After wiping his hands on the seat of his jeans, Luke dug into his hip pocket and took out his wallet. Extricating a couple of business cards, he slapped one down onto the table. 'Dale Gregg—loan officer at the bank where I stash my money…when I have any, and—' he tossed the second card down on top of it '—Elisa Thomson, a lawyer who's done some work for me recently. They both know my current financial status. I'll phone them as soon as I've fed Troy, and ask them to cooperate with Maxwell when he calls. They'll give him all the info you need.'

Whitney picked up the cards and read the addresses.

She looked up at him. 'You've been in California, all this time?'

'Land of surf and sun bunnies.'

'A beach bum.'

His only answer to her scornful comment was a slanting smile.

'So,' she went on, 'you've nothing to show for your thirteen years away but a tan, an empty bankbook, and—'

'And a baby.'

Whitney shook her head. 'Unbelievable.'

'Isn't he, though?'

'Unbelievable that someone with your potential could have screwed up so badly,' she snapped. 'It's commonplace to hear about the self-willed teenage girl who runs away from home because she refuses to live by the house rules—only to come back with her tail tucked between her legs and an illegitimate baby in her arms. It's unusual to see a reversal of roles…but your case is a perfect example—'

'You mean—' his blue eyes were wide and innocent '—someone took advantage of me and got me pregnant?'

'—and it's people like you who are ripping apart the very fabric of North American society—'

'Oh, I think that's a bit of an exaggeration! I'm only—'

'—with your irresponsible behavior! You want to have your fun, but when things go wrong, you want somebody else to bail you out. Bad enough you behave that way when you've only yourself to look after, but when you have a child—'

The baby whimpered.

Whitney jerked her head around and felt a stab of dismay. His little mouth was turned down, his lower lip was trembling and his tear-filled eyes were fixed on her with a look that said better than any words: 'How *could* you!'

Which was exactly what she asked herself.

How could she possibly have forgotten that Troy was in the room? She was well aware of how awful it was for a child to have to listen to grown-ups fighting, yet here she was, subjecting this one to that very thing.

'Babies,' Luke said quietly, 'pick up on bad vibes. When I'm around Troy, no matter how...difficult...things may be, I've always tried to maintain a happy and positive attitude. I'd appreciate it if you'd make an effort to do the same. The situation we're in isn't easy for either of us. Let's just try to make the best of it, mmm?'

A painful lump swelled in Whitney's throat, and though she tried to swallow it, it wouldn't go away.

Luke went to crouch by his son, running a hand over his dark hair, and speaking reassuringly to him. Soothing him.

Whitney picked up her mug and walked unhappily out of the kitchen.

And as she did, she swore that, however long Luke stayed at Brannigan House, no matter how he infuriated her, she'd never lose her temper with him again.

At least, she amended, not in front of the baby!

CHAPTER THREE

'EDMUND MAXWELL has gone on holiday and he won't be back for two weeks.' Whitney put her coffee mug into the dishwasher. 'That should give you a breathing space. Time to look around for a job. Once you've got one, you can move out.'

'A *job*?'

As she heard the amusement in Luke's voice, Whitney turned to glare at him. 'Yes, a job. As in "a paid position of employment?" Even beach bums have to grow up someday!'

'Not necessarily.' He shrugged and leaned back in his chair. 'Anyway, who'd hire me? I'm a high school dropout.'

'You could work as a laborer at a construction site—there's a new housing scheme going up at the end of the lake. You look fit enough—' she avoided looking at his wide chest and muscled arms '—and there should be no problem getting hired on.'

'Is there a bus service up here now from town?' Luke scratched his head. 'Didn't used to be…'

'You can eventually buy a used car.'

'What we have here is a catch-22 situation. If I were to find a job, I'd need a vehicle to get to it, but I wouldn't be able to afford a car till I had more than a few paychecks in my hand. Besides, there *is* a problem…'

Troy sputtered, and spat out a few crumbs of toast.

'—and as you can see,' Luke went on dryly, 'he's not about to be overlooked.'

'Enrol your son in a day care center. That's what other people in your position have to do. Why should you have to be any different!'

Troy was scowling, as he looked from one to the other.

A scowl which reminded Whitney of her vow not to fight with Luke in front of the child.

She drew in a deep breath. 'We'll continue this discussion later, when the baby's asleep.'

Luke got to his feet, and taking her arm in a firm grip, led her out into the hallway, letting the kitchen door swing shut.

'This discussion will go nowhere.' Tension tightened his voice. 'If you think I'd leave my son with a complete stranger, you've got rocks in your head.'

'No need to leave him with a stranger.' Whitney tilted her chin challengingly. 'Does the name Dixie Mae ring a bell?'

'Dixie who?'

'Five feet nothing, blond hair fluffed out to here, and breasts out to there?'

His quick grin irritated her. As did his lazily drawled, 'Ah, *now* I remember. Dixie Mae Best. She was—'

'One of your many girlfriends.'

'Dix's still around?'

'Oh, yes, she's still around. And she runs the Best Day Care Center in Emerald. She's had a couple of bad marriages, but apparently she's good with children.'

'Is she still as...?' Straight-faced, Luke sketched a couple of voluptuous circles with his hands.

'Why don't you look her up, and you can find out for yourself!'

'I may just do that. But I tell you one thing, I'll not put Troy in day care. The kid stays with me.'

'Well, that cuts down on your options. You really—'

He cut into her derisive response. 'Let's go for a walk.'

'A walk? I don't want to go for a walk! I have things to do.'

'When I was hiking up the road from town yesterday, I had a look at the vineyards. I want to have a closer look. And maybe you can explain why—'

'If you want to talk business, talk to Edmund Maxwell when he gets b—'

'The Emerald Valley Vineyard used to be one of the most profitable in the Okanagan. Don't try to tell me it still is. What we have here is a vineyard full of baco noir, verdelet, and Seyve-Villard—grapes my father planted sixteen years ago—grapes that have little cachet in today's varietal-driven market. Dammit, my grandmother should have seen what was happening! She should have anticipated—'

'Your grandmother had been failing for some time before her accident. She hired a temporary manager, but he didn't work out, and after that, she let things slide—'

'Didn't *you* take any interest in the vineyards? After all, it was Brannigan money that brought you up and has given you the high standard of living you enjoy here—'

'Now just a minute! When I was teaching, I contributed more than my fair share to the household expenses—'

'—and it'll be the interest from Brannigan capital that will in the future keep you in the luxury you're—'

'There *is* no Brannigan capital! Edmund Maxwell told me that yesterday, before he left. So you see, you have nothing to gain by standing in the way of my selling.'

'My grandmother used the *capital*? You've been living off the *capital*? My God, I can't believe—'

Whitney cringed from his burning anger and outrage. 'So you see, there's no option but to sell. Even if I wanted to, I couldn't afford to keep up this place.'

'Da-da-da...'

The plaintive call for attention came from the kitchen.

'Get a jacket.' Mouth set grimly, Luke glowered down at her. 'I want to take a closer look at what we've got. But I tell you now, you can forget about selling this place. It's not going to happen.'

Brannigan House was situated at the end of the northern tip of the Naramata bench. The vineyards, perched on the valley's steep slopes, with a south-western exposure, climbed above Emerald Lake. The neat rows striped the rolling hills like wales in heavy green corduroy.

Whitney had thrown on a parka over her T-shirt and jeans, but although Luke had dressed the baby cosily, and tucked the blue cap on his head, he himself wore no jacket.

Perhaps the carrier cut the breeze, at least on his back, Whitney reflected as they walked together down the road that cut diagonally across the planted vines.

'You say you've had nothing to do with the vineyards.' Luke didn't look at her as he spoke.

'Not because I wasn't interested,' she said steadily. 'It's just that with my fair skin, I can't stay out too long in the sun, so working outside was never an option for me—'

'Anyway, you were an academic.' He broke in roughly. 'Your nose was always stuck in one school text or another. Did you stay on at Penticton High?'

'For a year, then your grandmother sent me to boarding school on Vancouver Island. After graduation, I went to UBC...and before you start sniping, I waitressed part-time and paid all my tuition fees myself—'

'Ah. The University of British Columbia. So you...eventually...took my place...even there.'

'Your place was always open to you, Luke, if you'd wanted it.' She glanced a him, sideways, and saw that Troy had grabbed two handfuls of his father's sun-bleached blond hair and was enjoying a tug of war.

'Then what?' Luke asked. 'After UBC...'

'I took a year off to travel in Europe. And when I came home I got a job teaching English at Penticton High.'

'When do you go back?'

'I won't be going back.'

He glanced at her, his expression cynical. 'So you gave up your job in expectations of inheriting the Emerald Valley Vineyards? You thought you'd be a lady of leisure.'

'I gave up my job a year ago in order to look after your grandmother—'

'Didn't they keep your position open for you?'

'Are you completely out of touch with what's been going on in this province? Of course they didn't keep it open. When I left, they had dozens of applicants for the post.'

'So...you and I are in the same situation. No job, no prospects...but at least we have a roof over our heads.' Veering off the road, he started walking downhill, between the vines, and didn't resume their conversation.

Which suited Whitney just fine.

She followed him, pausing behind him when, from time to time, he stopped to inspect a vine, tug out a weed, pick some dry soil and let it run through his fingers, or examine a sagging overhead trellis.

On one such occasion, Troy threw back his head, and looked at Whitney upside down.

She smiled at him. What a little love he was! She made a soft coo-coo sound, for his ears alone, and he smiled back, charming her, and then he focused his attention once again on his father's hair.

After about ten minutes, Luke turned, so abruptly that Whitney almost walked into him.

'Let's go back,' he said. 'I've seen enough.'

'I'm going to walk on down to the lake.' At least

that way she would have some time on her own to think.

Troy gave a wide yawn.

'The baby should be in bed,' she went on quickly, afraid Luke might say he'd come with her. 'Do you need more blankets? You'll find some in the airing cupboard—it's upstairs, next to the—'

'I don't need a map to find my way around Brannigan House, Whitney.' His tone was harsh. 'I was born here. I know every nook and cranny, every cupboard, every—'

'Point taken. Only you don't need to be so nasty about it! You may have been born here...but I never asked to live here. At twelve years of age, I was given no choice in the matter. And—' her eyes sparked '—if I'd *had* a choice, this is the last place on earth I'd have chosen. You were the cruelest person I'd ever met, so wrapped up in your own jealousies and insecurities you never gave one thought to—'

'Didn't you suggest I stop hanging on to the past?'

His icy tone had the effect of a hard slap.

She brushed roughly past him and took off down the slope, her feet making quick padding sounds on the ground between the rows of vines.

She couldn't bear it; couldn't bear having him around.

And she'd changed her mind about one thing: She wasn't about to wait till Edmund Maxwell came back. After lunch, she'd drive into town, drop by his office and ask his partner to make the enquiries about Luke's financial state.

She'd hang around till the necessary calls were

made. And when she had the answer she confidently expected—that Luke had been lying about his barren bank account—then she'd drive straight home again, and tell him where to go.

And if he needed a lift to the nearest bus stop, she'd be more than willing to oblige.

It took only ten minutes to get to the lake.

Once there, she sought her favorite quiet spot, sheltered from the breeze, and sat down on the grass with her back against the trunk of a tree. Soon she became lost in her thoughts, thoughts that didn't include Luke.

They did include his grandmother.

At the funeral reception, Jack McKay, Cressida's doctor, had said to her, in an attempt to offer consolation, 'She was in a great deal of pain, Whitney. For her sake, be glad she is no longer suffering.'

And Cressida's best friends, Amelia Pitt and Martha Gray, had said, 'It's for the best, dear. And it's not as if it was unexpected. You must be glad it's all over. We know how hard it's been on you.'

Yes, the last year had been a hard one, but though she had many times been exhausted almost beyond endurance, after sitting up with Cressida through nights racked with agony, she knew she'd never be glad Cressida was gone. Glad for Cressida's sake perhaps, but not for her own. She was already missing her terribly.

And there, with no one to see or hear, but a couple of robins, several ducks bobbing closely by on the lake and a solitary black squirrel, at last she let the tears fall.

* * *

She didn't return to the house till noon.

And when she saw an unfamiliar station wagon parked at the front door, she uttered a small sound of exasperation.

Visitors. The last thing she needed. But even as she decided to veer around the side of the house and slip in the back way, the front door opened, and two people came out.

Luke...and Dixie Mae Best.

At the sight of the sexy blonde, Whitney almost stumbled. She'd always known Luke was a fast mover, but this was ridiculous!

They'd both seen her, unfortunately, and stifling a frustrated sigh, she rammed her hands into her parka pockets, and walked toward them.

'Miss McKenzie.' Dixie had been giggling as she came out the door, but as soon as she saw Whitney, her expression sobered. 'I was real sorry to hear about Mrs. Brannigan.'

'Thank you, Dixie.'

'Well.' The blonde glanced at her watch. 'I've gotta run. Luke, it was great hearing from you.' She smiled up at him. 'I'll have to tell Patsy—'

'Patsy Smith? She's still around, too?'

'Oh, sure...and Beth, and Liz, and Chantal McGee, and—oh, all the old gang! Laura Logan that was, and the Patterson twins and...' She grimaced. 'Even Begonia Bright.'

'Good old Begonia,' Luke said, laughing.

Dixie shook her head, and her heavily made-up eyes sparkled. 'I can't believe it—Luke Brannigan a daddy!'

Her hips swiveled under the thin fabric of her pink miniskirt as she walked over to her station wagon. Once inside, she rolled down the window, and as she pulled away, she called back to Luke, 'You call me now, y'hear?' And with a cheery wave she took off, leaving a cloud of dust in the air—and a sharper-than-ever tension between Luke and Whitney.

'Perhaps you should have waited a day or two,' Whitney said curtly, 'before making yourself so at home.'

'Oh, and why's that?'

But Whitney didn't answer. Suddenly aware that his gaze had narrowed and he was looking scrutinizingly at her face, she remembered her weeping bout, and wondered if her eyes were revealingly red-rimmed and swollen.

She stalked past him and ignoring his startled 'Hey, wait up!' marched into the house.

Making straight for the stairs, she went up to her room. She wasn't going to wait and eat lunch after all. She was no longer hungry...and *he* could fend for himself. The fridge was full of leftovers from yesterday's reception.

She was going to drive into town now, and talk to Edmund Maxwell's partner—his older brother Charles.

If she didn't get rid of Luke right away, she had a very strong feeling that she might come home someday very soon and find Dixie Mae Best ensconced in his bedroom...

Dixie Mae, Patsy Smith, Chantal McGee...and all

the 'rest of the old gang'...even including Begonia Bright!

'Luke was telling you the truth.' Charles Maxwell sat back in his swivel chair as he looked across his desk at Whitney. 'Both his lawyer and his banker have confirmed his story.'

Whitney felt a dull sinking sensation in the pit of her stomach as she rose unsteadily from her seat.

'So...I have to give Luke a home. And I can't sell the house, or the vineyards—'

'You could go to court, and contest the codicil.' Charles's knees creaked as he got to his feet.

'No. It's what Cressida wanted. I can never forget that if she hadn't taken me in after my mother died, I'd have ended up in a foster home. She didn't want me to turn Luke away if he needed somewhere to stay...and she would *never* have countenanced turning away a baby.'

She scooped up her purse from the floor, and swung the strap over her shoulder. 'Thank you very much, Mr. Maxwell. I appreciate your getting onto this so promptly.'

'Whitney.' The elderly man rounded his desk. 'Before you go...'

She paused. 'Mmm?'

'Luke's lawyer seemed to assume that I knew all about the events leading up to his present situation, and from what she said, I've gathered that Luke's marriage—'

'I don't want to know anything about that,' Whitney said in a rush. 'Bad enough that I've had to ask you to check out the truth of his story, without...delving further into his private life.'

'But it might help you understand Luke—'

'It's not necessary for me to understand him.' She touched the lawyer's arm, feeling the need to reassure him that if she was upset, he wasn't responsible. 'Now, you'll fill your brother in on what's been happening?'

'Of course. And if you've any more questions you need answering in the meantime, don't hesitate to call.'

As she walked out to the street, Whitney's mouth twisted in a wry smile. She wouldn't have been human if she didn't have questions. Of course she'd wanted to ask about Luke's marriage. She wanted to find out about his wife, wanted to know why she wasn't here with him...wanted to know why she wasn't caring for their baby. But she'd done the right thing, in cutting the lawyer off. She had to be able to face herself in the mirror each morning, and she couldn't have done that, not really, if she'd given in to the keen curiosity Charles Maxwell's words had ignited inside her.

'Would you mind telling me what you're doing?' Whitney planted her fists on her hips and glared at Luke's back and legs. That was all she could see of him. His head was hidden under the hood of the black pickup truck that had been stored in the garage for the past year, but was now sitting in the forecourt, its engine purring.

Luke obviously hadn't heard her approach, but as

she spat out her question, he lifted his head and at the sight of her, he straightened.

'Ah, you're back.' He swiped a hand over his brow, leaving behind a smear of oil. 'Who drove this pickup?'

'Your grandmother. Listen, you have no right to—'

'So it's been out of commission for a while. That explains it.' He shoved a rag into the hip pocket of his jeans. 'I've got it running smooth as a dream now. I saw you take off earlier in a flashy Mercedes. Your own car?'

'You were telling the truth.'

'I always do. But about what, in particular?'

'You're down and out.'

'Down,' he said grinning, 'but not out.' He patted the truck. 'If a man's got a set of wheels, he's never out.'

She wanted to remind him the truck was now hers; it came with the territory. She restricted herself to snapping, 'Good, now you'll be able to go look for a job.'

'Uh-uh. Not an option. I've told you I'm going to take care of Troy myself. No baby-sitters, no day care.'

'Then you're going to have a bit of a problem, aren't you, because not many females welcome an infant along on a date...and I can already see which way the wind is blowing! And don't think you can start asking your dates up here! You may—at the moment—live at Brannigan House, but there was nothing in that codicil that said you could bring your women to—'

'My women?' His lips quirked up at the edges.

His smugness increased her irritation with him.

'Your grandmother would be turning in her *grave* if she knew that within twenty-four hours of her funeral you'd invited Dixie Mae Best into her home. Good grief, you're not a randy seventeen-year-old any longer—it boggles my mind that you'd be—' She bit off the words that had danced to the tip of her tongue.

'What?'

She wiggled her shoulders frustratedly. 'I'm well aware of what that woman came up here for!'

'Dixie drove up here because I called her—'

'Tell me something I don't know!'

'And I called her because you said—'

'I said? What have I got to do with it?'

He grabbed her by the hand and pulled her around to the front of the truck. Troy was dozing, comfortably, in a baby car seat strapped snugly in place in the passenger seat.

'You said Dixie ran a day care center, and I figured if anybody could loan me a car seat, she'd be that one.'

For a long moment, Whitney stared at him, then flatly said, 'Oh.'

'Oh? Is that all?'

'Sorry.' The apology was grudging and barely audible. 'I just assumed—'

'What a naughty mind you have, Whitney McKenzie! And what a very exaggerated idea you have of my libido! I'm flattered that you think me such a Don Juan...but on the other hand—' his flippant tone had been replaced by one of harsh censure

'—it's insulting that you'd believe I'd be capable of that kind of sordid behavior.'

'You have a reputation,' Whitney retorted, unwilling to let him have the last word, 'so what else can you expect, other than that people will think the worst of you!'

'I expect you to take a look at the man I am now,' he said in a cutting tone. 'Just as I'm looking at the woman you've become...and I don't like what I see. But that doesn't surprise me. After all, you're your mother's daughter—'

Her palm was a mere inch from his face before she somehow controlled her primal urge to slap, but Luke was no mind reader...and his reaction was swift. Even as she made to pull back, he sliced up his hand and clamped her wrist.

His grip was inescapable. His eyes blazed fire.

'Don't ever try that again,' he said through clenched teeth, 'or I won't be answerable for the consequences—'

'I'm not afraid of you!' Challenge trembled in Whitney's voice. 'I might have been, thirteen years ago, but you can do *nothing* to me now—'

'Try this.'

He wrenched her toward him and in the space of a heartbeat his lips were on hers. Her mind reeled in shock, but to her dismay her senses sprang traitorously to life. Her breasts swelled as she tasted his dark hot flavor on her lips; and as his musky scent filled her nostrils, her nipples thrust out to rasp against the thin silk of her bra. The sensation was exquisitely pleasurable, indescribably erotic—

And absolutely intolerable.

In one savage movement, she jerked her wrist free of him and stumbled back. Her breathing was ragged; her hands clenched into fists at her side. 'You b—'

'Tit for tat.' He lifted his wide shoulders in a shrug. 'You want to be treated like a lady, act like one.'

'You provoked me!'

'And you didn't provoke me?'

'You started it!'

'Now who's acting like a child.' There was no mistaking his disgust. He turned away.

'This is not going to work.' She couldn't keep the edge of desperation from her voice.

He paused. Faced her again. 'What?'

'This. Our living together.'

'"If you can't take the heat, get out of the kitchen."'

'You surely don't expect *me* to leave?'

'The idea does have appeal. Actually I've been giving some thought to contesting my grandmother's will.' His smile was cold, and as cruel as it had always seemed to her as a child. 'It doesn't seem quite fair that you should end up with the Brannigan estate. The Emerald Valley Vineyards have always been a family affair, and you, Miss *McKenzie*, don't have one drop of Brannigan blood in your veins.'

CHAPTER FOUR

WHITNEY was in the kitchen around ten to six that evening when she heard Luke's firm tread outside in the corridor.

He'd been away all afternoon; she'd noticed the rumble of the truck as he took off down the road shortly after their quarrel.

Now he was back...

She stiffened in her seat, put down the sandwich she'd been eating and braced herself for his undoubted opposition to the plan she'd come up with in his absence—her plan to divide the house in two.

Into her rooms...and his rooms.

Her areas...and his areas.

With a rota—his hours and her hours—for common areas.

Adrenaline fizzed through her veins as she gazed tautly at the door.

It opened, and Luke breezed into the kitchen as if he owned it. He was laden down with bulging grocery bags.

'Hi.' His tone gave no indication of his mood.

'Where's Troy?'

He dumped the bags at the opposite end of the table from where she was sitting. 'I've just put him to bed.' He crossed to switch on the baby monitor.

Immediately the sound of sleepy gurgles murmured into the air.

'A van came by while you were out, with the delivery of some boxes for you. I had the driver put them upstairs in your room.'

'Yeah, I saw them. Thanks. Mostly just clothes and personal effects—mine and Troy's—stuff I packed up before leaving California.' His gaze flicked over Whitney's plate as he started unpacking his groceries. 'Working your way through the leftovers?'

'Mmm.' She picked up her unappetizing tuna sandwich and bit off a morsel. From under her lashes, she watched Luke drop a packet of steaks onto the table, followed by a roasting chicken, a slab of spareribs and a rack of lamb.

'So—' he glanced up '—which half of the fridge do you want? How about top shelves for you, bottom shelves for me. Same with the freezer section?'

Whitney felt as deflated as if he'd pricked her lungs and let out all the air...and she knew, by the ironic glint in his eyes, that he'd anticipated her strategy and had decided his best form of defense was attack. Well, this was one battle she was not going to let him win.

'Whatever.' As she spoke, one of his smaller bags—a brown paper one—toppled over, and several perfect mushrooms started rolling toward the edge of the table.

'And I was thinking.' Smiling smugly, he scooped up the mushrooms. 'Since you're such a late riser, I'll have the use of the kitchen first in the morning—say from seven till eight. And then again from noon till one, and in the dinner hour, from six till seven.'

'So...I'll have it for the rest of the day.' She put down the sandwich; another bite would surely choke her.

'Uh-uh—this is a three-way deal. You're forgetting about Troy, he has to eat, too. He's usually up by six, but since he's not yet on a regular schedule, his hours will be unpredictable.'

Whitney shoved back her chair and stumbled to her feet. 'So what you're saying is you want unlimited access to—'

'And then there's the rest of the house.' Absently Luke turned a tub of ice cream over in his hands. 'You can have the living room, I'll take the library—'

'But the TV's in the library—'

'You can't live without TV?'

'I can live without it. After all,' she said, adopting an airy tone, 'it won't be for long.'

'It may be for much longer than you imagine.' He bent down to stuff the ice cream tub into the freezer. 'I drove into Penticton this afternoon, got myself a lawyer.' He uncoiled himself and gazed at her challengingly. 'I'm going ahead with contesting my grandmother's will.'

Whitney felt as if a gigantic lead weight had dropped on her heart. Oh, how she hated fights. But she wasn't about to let Luke cow her, as she had when she was a frightened little twelve-year-old.

'You told me you were broke.' Her knuckles whitened as she gripped the back of her chair. 'But you've hired a lawyer. Where are you going to get the money to pay him?'

'Her.'

'Huh!' Whitney gave a scornful laugh. 'You've no financial assets so you used your physical ones to get what you wanted. Charming!'

'Tut-tut! So cynical for one so young! Actually Ms. Eaton—*Marilla*—has agreed to act for me on a contingency basis—you know,' he said slowly, deliberately, as if explaining something to a dim-witted child, 'if I win, she gets a percentage…if I lose, she gets zip.'

Whitney frowned. 'But…if you go ahead and contest the will, the estate'll be—'

'Frozen.'

'Which means you and I—'

'Will be living here, together, for quite some time.'

Intolerable.

Whitney drew herself to her full height of five feet five. 'If you think the prospect of a legal battle is going to intimidate me, you have another think coming. Cressida wanted *me* to have the estate. Why would a judge overturn—'

'There's no point in us second-guessing what a judge is going to decide. And that's in the future…let's focus on the present. We've divided the downstairs, let's divide the upstairs. The bedrooms. I'll stay in my present room, and Troy will have the use of my old room next door. Eventually I'll redecorate it, make it into a nursery—'

He was going too fast; she couldn't keep up with him. She felt her thoughts roil around in confusion.

'And,' he went on, '*your* rooms will be—'

'Off limits to you!' Lord, where had that shrillness come from? She'd barely recognized her own voice.

'Of course!' He presented his palms to her. 'Did I suggest anything else? Off limits, of course…until…'

'Until *what*?'

Turning his back on her, he opened the freezer door again and moved packages around to make space for the roasting chicken. 'Until you invite me in, sweetheart.'

The arrogance of the man! The unutterable gall! 'You're going to wait one heckuva long time for *that* to happen!' She sent a volley of invisible poisoned darts into his still-turned back. 'It may come as something of a shock to you that there's one woman in Emerald Valley who is totally immune to your charms—'

'Ah.' He swiveled around and threw her a *wicked* smile. 'So you do concede that I have charms?'

Frustration pounded her temples. 'You're impossible!' She snatched up her plate and stomped to the sink, where she swept her dilapidated sandwich into the garbage. 'And where did you get the money to buy all that food?' She whirled to face him accusingly as she spoke. 'You said you were—'

'When I was in town, I pawned my Rolex.' He shot out his left arm. 'See?'

'Yes,' she snapped, 'I see. How much did you get for it?'

'Enough…for the moment.' He stored away the lamb and the spareribs.

'And then?'

He ripped the cling film off the packet of steaks, and balling it, tossed it into the garbage pail under the sink. 'When I was up in the attic I came upon all the hockey memorabilia my grandfather left me—collectors' items now, and his stamp albums—worth a fortune today—'

'But you should be keeping those things for Troy!' The protest came out involuntarily. 'Surely—'

'"He must needs go *whom* the devil doth drive"!' Luke's tone mimicked—with uncanny accuracy—the tone she'd used on him earlier in the day when she'd corrected his misquote.

'Well, aren't *you* the quick study!'

'Yeah, not just a pretty face.' His grin was malicious. 'And now—' he veered a pointed gaze at the clock ticking tinnily on the electric stove '—it's six o'clock.'

She stared at him blankly.

'My dinner hour,' he drawled, taking a large onion from an orange mesh bag on the table. 'It begins now.'

'But—'

'You want to change the arrangements...already?'

'Of course not!' Her stomach rumbled; one dry tuna sandwich did not a dinner make. Her irritation increased till it was all she could do not to stamp her feet like a thwarted child. 'You can cook?' Despite her determination to remain aloof, her question came out...and sulkily.

'Yup.'

Curiosity drove her to ask her next question, one she didn't want to ask. 'Where did you learn?'

'In the kitchens of one very fancy hotel.'

'Oh.'

He quirked an eyebrow. 'Anything else?'

'No.' She waved a hand toward the stove, and hoped the gesture looked indifferent. 'It's all yours.'

'Thank you.'

'You're welcome!'

But her sarcastic retort went unheard. He had already turned on the extraction fan above the burners, and its loud humming drowned out every other sound.

Steak and onions. That was what he was going to have for dinner.

Her mouth watered.

And her resolve stiffened.

The battle was on.

Whitney went upstairs to brush her teeth and rid her mouth of the taste of tuna; but on passing Luke's open bedroom doorway, she was irresistibly drawn to steal into the room and spend a few moments with the baby.

Troy was sitting in the middle of his crib, engrossed in trying to nest one yellow plastic cup inside a slightly larger red one. He glanced up as she approached, and stared unblinkingly as she said, 'Hi, there, sweetie pie.'

For the longest time he just gazed up at her with his huge blue eyes, not uttering a sound...almost as if he were deciding whether or not she was worthy of his friendship.

Apparently she passed inspection.

He dropped the cups, and gripping the vertical rails of the crib, with much puffing and grunting he hauled himself unsteadily to his feet.

And reached out to clutch a handful of her hair.

'You really like my hair, don't you,' she said, with a laugh as he tugged a thick red strand and tried to drag it into his mouth. 'Well, I like yours, too.' She ran her fingertips lightly over his crown, admiring the exquisite fineness of his hair even as she breathed in the wonderful baby scent that came from his head. 'You're such a love,' she murmured, and gave a wry grin. 'How come someone so sweet can have such a bad-tempered old man for a father!'

Troy chuckled, as if he could understand her.

She glanced around, and shook her head. Even without the four huge boxes that the driver had brought up in the afternoon, the room would have still looked as if a bomb had exploded in it. The old duffel bag lay beside Luke's dresser, with clothes trailing from it. The bed was unmade, and several of Troy's tiny items of clothing were scattered on the carpet. She resisted the itch to clear up. Luke needn't think she was going to take over tidying his room; if he wanted to live in a pigsty, that was his choice.

'Your poppa,' she said, turning her attention again to Troy, who had now lost interest in her hair, and had dropped down onto his bottom again, 'is not only bad-tempered, he is messy. Besides which, he is rude, and arrogant...and when he was a teenager, he had every girl in the valley chasing after him...except me! He was a heartbreaker of the worst kind...but even when I was twelve, I detested him.'

Troy scowled, and she raised her eyebrows.

'You think I'm being too hard on him? You want me to say something *good* about your old man? Well, tell you what,' she said, as she turned to go, 'if I can ever *find* something good to say about him, I promise you'll be the first to know. But don't hold your breath…'

'Last night,' Luke said when she came into the kitchen next morning, 'I came up with a plan.' He dried the slatted microwave dish grasped in his big hand before storing it away in the cupboard.

The fragrant smell of bacon still hung in the air…along with the smell of coffee; but the pot, Whitney saw, was empty. Washed…and ready for her to use. Why couldn't he have made enough for two!

She hid a sigh. She had thought about making a request for that very thing, the night before. She'd bumped into him at the bottom of the stairs as she was on her way to bed, and she was actually about to *lower* herself to ask him, when he said, with a decidedly malicious smirk,

'I would be less than a perfect gentleman, Whitney, if I didn't warn you that when you're chatting to my son, while he's in his crib, everything you say is clearly relayed to me through his baby monitor.'

She gaped…and felt her cheeks turn scarlet. What had she said?

His smile was mocking. 'Nothing good, I can assure you. But don't worry about it…the feeling's mutual.'

She'd stumbled off upstairs, feeling more stupid than she'd felt in her life. And because of it, had barely slept. So now, she wasn't only more tired than usual, but her nerve endings were screaming out in frustration: *Caffeine*!

'Did you hear me? Are you with me?' Luke passed a hand across her eyes. 'I said...last night I came up with a plan—'

He'd already found out she wasn't a morning person. He was about to find out she wasn't livable with till she'd had her first mug of coffee.

'And yesterday,' she snapped as she snatched a filter from the package, '*we* came up with a plan. And that plan included your being out of the kitchen by eight.'

'Is it eight already?' His blue eyes were guileless. 'It's a pain, having no watch!'

'There's a clock on the stove!'

'Well golly gee, I'd forgotten about that!'

She ignored the laughter in his tone and looked around suspiciously. 'Where's Troy?' Was Luke going to announce that he was about to give his son his breakfast? Was he going to be hanging around in here even longer?

'He's upstairs playing in his crib. Look—what I have to say won't take very long. We can talk while you eat breakfast.'

'There's no point in having rules if we don't keep them! Besides, I don't eat breakfast.' Tugging open the fridge, she looked for the green tin where she kept the ground coffee. She always tucked it in the bottom shelf of the door. It wasn't there.

She swiveled around and glared at him. 'Did you touch my coffee?'

'It's right there, on the top shelf of the door.'

'If you use my stuff, please put it back where you—'

'But the bottom half of the fridge is mine. Remember?'

He was using that voice again, that reasonable, soothing voice he'd use to a recalcitrant child. She bit off the rude word that bounced to her lips.

She took out the tin, clicked open the lid, measured three scoops into the filter, before returning the can to the fridge.

'Sorry isn't in your vocabulary?' His tone was mild.

Keeping her back to him, she poured cold water into the coffeemaker, and plugged it in. 'You're not even supposed to *be* in the kitchen right now.'

She looked out the window…but what caught her eye was not the fresh spring scene outside, but Luke's reflection in the glass. She'd already noticed he was wearing a blue T-shirt that made his eyes dazzle, and black cords. Now, despite her sour mood, she had to admit he'd never looked more attractive.

Nor had the kitchen ever seemed smaller.

She saw his mouth twist in a smile, and realized he'd become aware of her scrutiny.

She turned, folded her arms across her emerald green shirt and stared at him defiantly, willing him to leave.

'Okay.' He started toward the door. 'But first, I'll give you food for thought. We're going to be stuck here together for months—'

'Don't count on it!'

'—perhaps even years.' He stopped right in front of her, so close she could smell his spicy aftershave and could almost feel the heat of his skin. 'We've got to do something about the vineyards. I have a suggestion, but you'll have to cooperate if it's going to work. When can we talk?'

Certainly not now. My brain turns to mush when you stand so close. 'Later.'

'Later…when?'

'After I've had my first cup of coffee.'

'Ah, you're one of those, are you!'

'One of *what*?'

'When you've poured your *second* cup—' the corners of his mouth tilted tauntingly '—come to the library. I'll outline my plan.' He scooped the baby monitor on his way out.

'*One of what*?' she repeated, her mood becoming more irritable by the second.

But the door was already swinging shut behind him, and her only answer was the echo of his mocking laugh.

'Come in!'

At Luke's response to her firm *rat-tat* on the library door, Whitney pushed the door open and entered the room.

He was standing at the window, looking out over the valley and the vineyards. He didn't turn right away.

Mug in hand, shc crossed to sit down on a leather ottoman in front of the gas fire. The flames leaping from the fake logs sent out a glow of warmth. She stretched out her long legs in front of her.

'So.' She cupped her hands around the floral china mug. 'What's this plan you want to talk about?'

He turned, and crossed to Cressida's carved Chinese desk. Dropping into the chair behind it, he tilted the legs back and clasped his hands behind his head. 'Supposing I hadn't come on the scene.' Eyes half-shut, he scrutinized her lazily. 'What would you have done with the estate?'

'Guess I'd have had to sell.'

'Sounds as if you wouldn't have wanted to.'

'Of course I wouldn't! This has been my home for the past thirteen years. All my roots are here—'

'Okay, no need to get your back up. So you'd have put the property up for sale because—'

'Because I don't have enough money to keep it going. You yourself said the vineyards aren't a viable proposition the way they are.'

'So you'd sell, because you could see no other option. At least, no option you could afford.'

'If I had enough money,' Whitney took a sip of her coffee and relished the surge of life it zipped through her veins, 'I could hire a manager, and we could rip out those veins and replant the vineyard—'

'But it would be about five years before you got a full crop on the new vines.'

She lifted her shoulders in a shrug. 'I'm well aware that given my financial situation, replanting wouldn't be an option.'

He tipped the chair forward, and folded his arms on the desk. His blue gaze fixed her with a steely intensity.

'There is another option,' he said.

Her own gaze was skeptical. 'What's that?'

'Grafting cuttings from vines whose grapes are now

high in demand, onto existing hybrid roots. Up until a few years ago, it was never done in the Okanagan—at least, not successfully.'

'Why the failure?'

'It was put down to the climate here...to the bitter cold of our winter climate.'

'And that wasn't it?'

'One of the more progressive vineyard owners decided that the failure might not be due to the climate, but to the fact that those who were doing the grafting weren't skilled in the technique. So he brought experienced grafters up from the States and let them loose on half his acreage—'

'And the success rate?'

'Amazing. And if we graft this spring, we could pretty well count on having a full crop in the fall of next year. The initial costs either way—grafting or replanting—are about the same in year one. But after that, the savings on the production side would be solid, and the difference in cash flow staggering. So...what do you think?'

His enthusiasm was infectious, but Whitney deliberately tamped down her rising excitement. 'It's pointless to discuss it, since we have no money. Apart from everyday running expenses, money would be needed to buy the cuttings for grafting—'

'Yes of course—'

'And grafters would have to be hired. Experienced ones. How would we pay their wages?'

Luke's eyelids flickered...and Whitney slowly put down her coffee mug. She sensed he'd anticipated her question, and had already come up with an answer—

an answer she wouldn't like. The tension in the room tightened.

'Well?' she prodded warily.

'The Mercedes,' he said. 'It's in your name?'

'Yes, it is. But why...?'

'My grandmother bought it for you?'

In a defensive tone, she said, 'It was a graduation gift, when I came home with my Masters.'

'I'm not sniping. I'm trying to determine what your assets are.'

'The Merc is mine,' she said stiffly. 'It's just two years old. You can guess what it's worth.'

'And what do you have in your bank account?'

'Only a couple of thousand dollars.' Where was this inquisition leading?

His eyes became unfocused, and she could almost hear the gears working in his mind. When she could bear the silence no longer she waved an impatient hand in front of his face.

'Earth to Brannigan. Earth to—'

'Sorry.' His hair glinted like gold as he scratched a hand abstractedly through the blond strands. 'I was trying to figure out costs, and we could make a start, graft half the vines this spring, and then next spring—yes, I think—'

Finally figuring out why he was so interested in the value of her car, Whitney rose abruptly to her feet.

'What *I* think,' she snapped, 'is that you're taking far too much for granted!' Her hands were fisted, but she kept them pressed to her sides, though she was dearly tempted to lash out at him. 'The plan you've concocted may well appear feasible to you, but it seems I'm the one who has to make the sacrifices. I sell *my* car, we use *my* money, we live in what's at present *my* house!' Her upper lip curled in a sneer. 'Just what do *you* plan to do, besides being a parasite!'

He surged to his feet and glowered at her. 'Just hang on a minute—'

'And what do I get out of it at the end of the exercise, if the judge declares that will invalid! Zip! I walk away with nothing but the shirt on my back—'

'Which was *exactly* what you walked in here with thirteen years ago!'

The sudden silence was so thick she felt it choke her. She stared shakily back at him. At his grimly set features, the hostility in his eyes, the rigid set of his shoulders.

'That,' she said quietly, 'was a low blow. But at least I've done something with myself, these past years. I'm proud of what I've accomplished. And your grandmother was proud of me, too. I've told you before, Luke, you can't hurt me anymore. The only person you're hurting, with your cheap shots, is yourself.'

She turned and walked away from him, every line of her body spelling out her rejection of him…and of his ideas.

How ironic it was that when she'd seen him so excited by his plan, she'd felt a nagging self-doubt over depriving him of his birthright. But his outburst of hostility to her had swiftly dispelled that pricking of her conscience; and as a result, the whole fabric of his plan lay in tatters.

CHAPTER FIVE

THE IMPASSE might have gone on for weeks had it not been for Dixie Mae Best.

The blonde phoned several evenings later, while Luke was upstairs bathing Troy. Whitney picked up the phone in the living room, and when she heard the familiar husky voice at the other end of the line, she stiffened.

'I'm sorry, Luke's busy right now,' she said. 'I'll have him call you back.'

'No, don't hang up, Miss McKenzie—it's you I want to speak to!'

'Me?'

'Patsy Smith and Chantal McGee and the rest of the gang...even Begonia Bright...we were all talking about Luke, and we decided to have him over for a shower.'

A shower. Oh, she could just see it—all those naked bodies glistening under a stinging hot spray of sparkling water. Luke...and the entire gang. Enough of them that they might well make the *Guinness Book of Records* for the largest number of people squeezed into one shower stall at the same time—

'Miss McKenzie? Are you still there?'

Whitney sank onto the nearest chair. 'Yes,' she said faintly, 'I'm still here. This shower—'

'A baby shower, that is. For little Troy.'

'Oh.' Whitney rolled her eyes. *That* kind of shower.

'Listen, I don't have time to talk right now, I'm on my way over to Hetty's to decorate the salon—she's letting us use it for the party. What I need for you to do, is to get Luke and the baby to Hetty's tomorrow night at six-thirty—'

Whitney had the odd feeling that she was being mowed over by a steamroller. 'I can't *possibly*—'

'You already got plans?'

'No. No, but…Luke and I…we're not even talking to each other! How on earth would I be able to—'

'A smart lady like you, with a string of degrees tacked after your name—you'll find a way!'

Whitney opened her mouth to say very firmly, absolutely definitely, that she was going to do no such thing, when Dixie said quietly, 'That poor kid, he's had a helluva start to his life so far, hasn't he?'

Her husky voice had sounded close to tears. Whitney felt goose bumps rise on her skin. What on earth did Dixie mean? She obviously assumed Whitney knew what she was talking about. But even as Whitney struggled to make sense of it, the blonde went on softly,

'So you can see why we all want to fuss over the little tyke…make him feel loved and wanted. We're all counting on you, Miss McKenzie, tomorrow night. Don't let us down.'

Before Whitney could find her voice, the other woman had hung up…leaving a host of unanswered questions behind her.

At four o'clock the following afternoon, Whitney went in search of Luke. She found him in the kitchen.

He'd apparently just come in from a walk in the rain with Troy; the child was sitting on the floor, his cheeks ruddy, and Luke was whisking off his tiny red rubber boots.

He must have heard her come into the kitchen, but he ignored her—just as they'd been ignoring each other since their quarrel several days before.

She wanted to stomp right out again. Why was she doing this? she asked herself testily.

But it wasn't for him. It was for the baby.

Holding that thought, she forced out the words that were digging their heels into her throat.

'I have a favor to ask you.'

Tugging off Troy's waterproof jacket, Luke lifted his son up into his high chair. 'Yeah?' He fastened the straps and snapped the tray back in place.

'I have an appointment at Hetty's Beauty Salon later on, to have my hair cut.' A lie, but a white and necessary one. 'And there's something wrong with my car.' Another lie. 'I tried it earlier, and it won't start.'

'You want me to check it out?' He turned and looked at her. His blue eyes held not one hint of friendliness; it was like being looked at by a stranger. 'Sure. I can—'

'No!'

He raised his brows.

'I don't want you fiddling around with my car. I've already phoned a garage in Penticton.' Lie number three. 'And they're sending a mechanic out tomorrow morning—'

'It could be something simple, such as—'

'Will you, or will you not, give me a drive?'

'How can I refuse—' his tone was sardonic '—since you ask so prettily?'

'Thank you.' She sounded positively shrewish. 'I need to be there at six-thirty.' She turned to leave.

'Your hair doesn't need cutting.'

She froze. Had he sensed that she was lying?

'It's beautiful, just as it is. Why the hell would you want to cut it?'

The rasping edge to his voice scraped her nerves and sent shivery tingles dancing through her body. Why did a compliment from him come out sounding like an insult? She ignored it anyway. 'I'll have to ask you to pick me up again afterward,' she said coolly. 'Can you find something to do in Emerald, for an hour or so?'

He took an apple from the fruit basket on the table. 'I'll call on Dixie Mae.' He crunched his strong white teeth into the apple. 'She'll be happy to see me.'

'What an excellent idea! But you'd best give her a call to let her know you're coming—that way, she'll have time to lay out the red carpet!'

At six-thirty sharp, Luke pulled the truck up outside a white frame house at the far end of Emerald; a house with a wide carport, a canary yellow door and an ancient neon sign that told the world this was the home of Hetty's eauty Salo.

'So.' Luke switched off the engine, and sat back in his seat, his hands sprawled over the steering wheel. 'Hetty still has her salon set up in the basement of her place?'

'That's right.'

'I'm surprised that you patronize such a humble establishment.'

Whitney murmured a noncommittal 'Mmm.' She wasn't about to volunteer the information that she'd never in her life set foot inside Hetty's.

Luke got out, and came around to help her down from the truck's high seat, his hand cupping her elbow firmly.

As usual, his closeness made her feel as if she was about to hyperventilate. 'Did you…phone Dixie?' she asked, and then was annoyed at the breathiness of her voice.

'No. I'm going to drive home and come back for you.'

Luke's hand was still clasped around her elbow. Unnecessarily. And the hardening pressure of his fingers as he stared down at her was sending electrical messages sparking between them. Did he feel it, too, this chemistry? His quickened breathing was her answer.

She tugged her elbow free and stepped back. 'That seems such a waste of gas. Why don't you come in—I won't be long—and I'm sure Hetty'll give you a cup of coffee. Besides, she'd love to see Troy.'

'No, I don't w—'

'Oh, come on,' she said impatiently, 'don't be such an old stick-in-the-mud. It's not going to kill you to hang around for a while…and it'll give Hetty a kick to see you. Get Troy—I'll wait in the carport, out of the rain.'

Without giving him time to reply, she walked

smartly away from him. She thought she heard a sputtered oath…and when a few moments later, the door of the truck slammed shut, she thought she'd failed in her mission. But just as she reached the carport, she became aware of Luke's heavy tread coming fast along the driveway behind her.

She felt the knotted muscles in her shoulders relax. So, she hadn't failed after all…and as soon as she had delivered him safely to the party, she could slip away.

When she rang the bell, Hetty came to the door. The hairdresser was wearing a clinging white rib-knit sweater, and polyester dress pants the same shiny jet black as her beehive hairdo. Her brown eyes shone and her scarlet lips widened in a smile as she welcomed them.

'Come in, honey!' She gave Luke a huge hug that included Troy. 'Let me see this baby I've been hearing so much about from Dixie Mae. Oh, isn't he precious!'

Over Luke's shoulder, she gave Whitney a thumbs-up sign. 'Now let's go down these steps, to the basement.'

'My salon's right along there,' she added when they reached the foot of the narrow stairway. 'Follow me.' With a quick bouncing gait, she led them along the hallway to a closed door, which she pushed open before stepping aside.

'Go right in, Luke, I've a fresh pot of coffee waiting.' And with that, she shoved the unsuspecting Luke forward, into the brightly lit and garishly decorated salon.

In unison, shrilly excited female voices chorused, 'Surprise!'

An obviously confused Luke muttered 'What the...?'

And Hetty said happily, 'It's a party, Luke honey, for Troy. A baby shower.'

From her position in the hallway, Whitney could see about fifteen females crowded around Luke, queuing up for a hug, laughing, some wiping tears from their eyes. Dixie Mae stood a little apart, smiling—like a mother hen, with all her brood together and getting along for once!

The sight was a heartwarming one. And it moved Whitney to an extent that surprised her.

As a child, she'd hated Luke because he'd always been so cruel to her. Yet at that same time in his life, despite his wild teenage escapades and his reputation as a hellion and a heartbreaker, he'd obviously been adored by these girls—women now—who had gone to high school with him.

And he still held a warm place in their affections.

Thrown off balance by her mixed feelings, Whitney turned away and quickly retraced her steps.

Quietly she closed Hetty's front door behind her and then scooted along the driveway to the truck. If Luke needed a drive home, he would call her; but she imagined that Dixie Mae had already delegated somebody—probably herself!—to chauffeur the guest of honor home.

She clambered up, slammed the door shut and jingled through her bunch of keys till she found the right one. Poking it into the ignition, she switched it on.

It was a couple of years since she'd used the truck, so she took a minute or two to ascertain the location and purpose of each switch on the dash. Eventually she found the knob for operating the windshield wipers, and she switched them on. She adjusted the rearview mirror. And had just put her hand on the gear-shift, about to change from Park to Drive—

When somebody yanked the door open.

With a gasp, she jerked her head around.

To find Luke standing there in the rain, just inches away, getting soaked. And as she gaped, he reached over, switched off the engine and pocketed the key.

'No way!' He shook his head. 'No bloody way. You got me into this…you'll stay and suffer through it, too. A hen party!' His lips twisted wryly. 'Good grief, woman—'

He grasped her arm and despite her protests, hauled her down. 'Come on.' He slammed the door. 'Hetty's waiting. They all expected you to stay. They wanted you to.'

'But I didn't bring a present, for the baby—'

'I'm to be sitting in some kind of a throne! I need you to hold Troy…he's shy, with all those strangers…'

How could she argue with that? Besides, she was no match for Luke, physically; if she didn't walk, she had the distinct feeling he would sweep her up and carry her in.

'Well!' She gave a rueful laugh. 'What are we waiting for? Let's get inside before we catch pneumonia!'

'Attagirl!' He grasped her hand tightly, and like a

couple of children, they ran up the driveway together, splashing heedlessly through puddles as they went.

With the rain in her face, and her hand in his, Whitney felt an odd wild drumming in her blood…and the kind of giddy happiness she hadn't known for a very long time.

'Thanks, guys, for a great party!'

As Luke leaned out of the window of the departing truck, and waved to the group assembled in Hetty's carport, Whitney sank back in her seat and smiled.

It had, indeed, been a great party. She'd drunk cheap champagne, eaten store-bought cake iced with chocolate frosting—and cuddled a sleepy Troy in her lap as Luke, in an oversize gold foil crown and a white frilly apron, was presented with gifts for his son; and was congratulated later by one and all for being 'such a darned good sport.'

Once the truck had left the environs of Emerald and they were driving up the side road leading to Brannigan House, he said, out of the blue,

'You owe me one.'

'A present for Troy? Yes, I know—'

'Not a present for Troy. You owe me one for tricking me tonight.' His hands on the steering wheel were steady. 'Devious, McKenzie. Very devious.'

'So…what did you have in mind?'

'A simple request.'

'Yes?'

'Listen to my plan for the vineyard. Hear me out—this time, without flying off the handle and—'

'I didn't fly off the handle! I was perfectly cool, calm and—'

'On the surface. Underneath, your pot was boiling over.'

He was right, of course. She'd been beside herself with anger. And though she'd tried not to think about the bind she was in, worry about the future still lurked like a dark monster in the back of her mind.

'Okay. I'll listen. But I'm not promising anything.'

'Just listen,' he said. 'That's all I ask.'

When they got home, Luke went upstairs to put Troy to bed.

Whitney took off her jacket and hung it in the closet. With her gaze fixed on her reflection in the mirrored door, she slipped a small brush from her purse and drew it through her damp hair. Her cheeks were flushed, and her eyes looked huge, and luminous, the clarity of the green startling. Luke had apparently been able to read her anger in them when they'd quarreled. Was he able to read every other emotion there, too? It was an alarming thought...

She'd have to be very careful. If he guessed how vulnerable she was to his sexual magnetism, he would surely take advantage of that vulnerability.

She was just slipping the brush back into her bag when she heard Luke's voice, coming from the stairs.

'I'm glad,' he said, 'that you weren't really planning to have it cut.'

Heart lurching, she clicked her bag shut and turned from the mirror. 'Is Troy asleep?'

'It really is very beautiful.' He'd reached the foot

of the stairs. 'As a rule, I'm not partial to redheads, but in your case—'

'Whether or not you're partial to redheads is of absolutely no interest to me.' Her coolly dismissive tone made it quite clear he needn't pursue *that* line of conversation further! She started toward the living room. 'We can talk in here. I'll just fix the fire first.'

She wasn't aware that he was right behind her till she was at the side of the hearth, leaning over to open the lid of the log box, and she felt his hand on her shoulder.

'I'll do that,' he murmured. 'You sit down.'

She sank onto a comfy low-slung love seat, and wriggling off her sneakers, curled into a corner with her feet tucked under her. Warily she watched as he arranged a few logs on the still-glowing embers.

He stared down at the sparks and licking flames for a moment, and dusted his hands together before turning around.

'You want something to drink?' he asked.

'No, thanks. But you go ahead.'

He shook his head. 'So...did you have a good time tonight?'

'Yes, I did.'

His gaze narrowed. 'You don't really know Hetty, do you...or the rest of the crowd.'

'After your grandmother came out of hospital, Hetty came up once a week to do her hair. Till then...no, I hadn't really known her. When I was a little girl, Cressida used to drive me to her hairdresser in Penticton.'

'And Dixie Mae—'

'They were all in their final year at high school, when I was in Grade 7. We traveled in the same school bus, but they never paid me any attention. I used to watch them, though. Used to envy them, actually.' Her smile had a sardonic twist. 'As you yourself said, in those days I had legs like twigs and hair the color of carrots. They all looked so glamorous—especially Dixie Mae, with her blond hair and her flashy clothes and her—you know!' Mockingly she copied Luke's earlier gesture, when he'd sketched a couple of voluptuous circles with his hands.

'But you didn't like them, did you—that gang.'

'They were part of your crowd, so...no, I didn't like them. Besides, they were loud, and brash, and—'

'And now?'

'They're still loud and brash...but underneath it all, they're a nice bunch, Luke. They went out of their way to make me feel comfortable.'

'They were a bit wary of you at first but...they liked you, too. I could see it.'

Embarrassed by the sudden intensity in his voice, Whitney said, lightly, 'What's not to like!'

He was staring at her—almost as if he was asking himself that very question. But then he shook his head as if to clear his thoughts, and she knew that whatever answer he'd come up with, he wasn't about to share it.

Instead he dropped into a chair opposite her. Knees apart, he rested his forearms on his thighs and pinned her with his dazzling blue gaze.

'I know,' he said, 'that you're concerned about selling your car and sinking the proceeds into the vineyard, but I assure you that whatever the outcome of the trial, you won't lose, financially.' He leaned forward. 'Do you trust me?'

She paused, but only for a second. 'So far, you've never given me any reason not to.'

'Okay. Then here's the plan. I'll have my lawyer draw up a contract that will guarantee that you get back every dollar of your investment, with interest, in the event that the hearing goes in my favor.'

'If the will's declared invalid, do you automatically inherit the estate?'

'If it's declared invalid, a prior will would become valid. According to Maxwell, there *was* no prior will. My grandmother apparently refused to accept that she was one day going to die—'

'But her accident, coupled with the discovery of her tumor, obviously changed her thinking. She wrote the will just a couple of days after she got out of hospital, at a time when she was very weak and her spirits at a low ebb.' Unhappy memories started to crowd into Whitney's mind; with an effort, she closed them out. 'Go on,' she said. 'If there's no other will, what happens?'

'Then my grandmother would have been considered to have died intestate. And since she wasn't survived by a husband or child, then the estate would devolve to her grandchild.'

'You.'

'Yeah.'

He seemed so confident of winning, Whitney reflected, but where was the strength in his position? She couldn't see it. But as she turned the matter over in her mind, she began to feel a vague uneasiness. She'd just told Luke she trusted him...but how far would he go to get what he wanted?

'Whitney?'

'Sorry.' She jerked her thoughts into place. 'To get back to your plan for the vineyards...your contribution would be...what?'

'My contacts. My expertise. And my hard work.'

'Contacts?'

'I was born and brought up here, Whitney. I know a lot of people in the industry. I've already had an exploratory talk with Victoria Moss of the Sagebrush Vineyards, about her supplying us with pinot blanc and pinot gris clones. She's also open to considering extending us a line of credit.'

'And your expertise?'

Luke's laugh was dry. 'I started working here in the vineyards at the age of two, when I was old enough to tug out my first weed! By the time I was twelve, I was capable of doing everything from repairing trellises to spraying the vines to driving the vineyard tractors. And all through high school, I spent every summer working in the fields—'

'But that's a long time ago! Surely since then, both methods and equipment have become modernized—'

'For the past several years I've been working in vineyards in the Napa Valley. In particular I've done a lot of grafting, learned from the experts—'

'You said you'd been a beach bum!' Indignantly Whitney glared at him.

'*You* said that. All I said was that California was

the land of sea and surf bunnies. You assumed…the rest.'

'Well, that still doesn't make you look much better! If you'd been watching your money, you wouldn't have had to come back here without a cent in the bank.'

He didn't respond to her jibe. Instead he went on, 'And thirdly, I'll work like the devil to get this place back on its feet again. I'll hire experienced grafters to come up from California, and we'll also get a crew of locals, but I'll be out there myself from the crack of dawn every day, seven days a week—'

'Aren't you forgetting something?' Whitney broke in stiffly. 'Or rather…some*body*?'

Luke had been so intent on what he was saying that when she interrupted him, he stared at her, blankly, for a moment. And then he said, 'Troy?' He shook his head. 'No, of course I'm not forgetting Troy.'

'But you've always sworn you wouldn't put him in day care, so…who's going to look after him, while you're out in the fields?'

'You.'

'*Me*?'

'He's taken to you—didn't you see that this evening, at Hetty's? They all wanted to hold him…but you were the one he kept turning to. You've told me that your chances of getting a teaching job right now are nil, and with the summer break just a couple of months away…' He lifted his wide shoulders in a 'What's left to argue about?' gesture.

Slowly Whitney rose to her feet. 'You've covered every base, haven't you!'

He got up, too, and he towered over her. 'So.' His eyes had a bright, hard glint. 'You'll go along with it?'

She wanted to step back, out of reach of his powerful aura, but she forced herself to stay where she was.

'I'm not saying that.' She felt her neck crick as she looked up at him. 'But I *will* think it over.'

'Don't wait too long. If we're going to do it, we have to get going without delay—April's the best time for grafting. Whitney, I owe my grandmother, for all those years I was away. I feel…driven…to make a success of the vineyard, as a tribute to her memory. Besides, I'll be damned if I'll let our vines become obsolete…and that's what's going to happen, unless we combine forces…'

Combine forces.

The words trembled in the air between them.

'I'll let you know in the morning.' Whitney struggled against the invisible hand that was pressed to the small of her back, pushing her toward him. 'I'm…off to bed now.'

She wanted to put her hands up to his face, touch her fingers to his cheeks, draw his mouth down to cover hers. She found herself gazing at his mouth. Beautiful, sensual, tempting. Barely aware of what she was doing, she ran the tip of her tongue over her own upper lip.

'You're asking for trouble.' His voice was silky. 'Don't do that…and don't look at me like that…unless you're prepared to follow through.'

Follow through? Oh, she knew only too well what

he meant…and the last thing in the world that she was going to do was sleep with this man.

Cheeks blazing, she spun away from him and made for the door.

If she did in the end decide to combine forces with Luke, she'd make sure the liaison between them would be purely a business one. To combine forces with him in a *sexual* liaison could lead to only heartbreak and disaster.

Luke was putting some plates away when she walked into the kitchen the next morning.

'Help yourself to coffee,' he said absently.

Her gaze flicked to the coffeemaker, and she saw the pot was half-full. Blessed man, he'd actually made extra.

She poured a mugful, stirred in sugar and wasted no time taking that first sip. 'Mmm.' She savored the start-up kick the caffeine gave her system. 'Thanks.'

'You're welcome.'

Troy was sitting in his high chair, his face smeared with porridge, his wide blue gaze fixed unwaveringly on her. Whitney set down her mug and crossed over to greet him with a cheery 'Hi, there, sweetie pie…how are you today?'

'Ma-ma-ma!' His gaze drifted to the gold barrette she'd used to pull her hair to one side. He dropped his spoon and lunged out for the shiny clasp.

Whitney swayed out of reach of his sticky hands.

'Hey!' she said and laughed softly. 'That's a no-no!' She glanced at Luke. 'He's a—'

She halted abruptly when she saw the glitter of sexual awareness she'd surprised in his gaze. A shiver skimmed her nerves. She had the unnerving feeling he'd been undressing her with his eyes—and enjoying every delicious glimpse.

Knees wobbling, she fetched a cloth from the sink, wiped off Troy's hands...and ordered her heart to be still.

'There.' She cleaned a lump of porridge from the child's hair, and deliberately stood back to admire him. 'My,' she said, 'what a handsome fella you are!'

'Like father, like son.'

Luke's tone had been amused, and drawing in a tight breath, Whitney risked a fleeting glance in his direction. His expression, she noted with relief, no longer held any sexual undertones; it had, in fact, become teasing.

'Right,' she said with artificial lightness, 'you're a handsome pair, there's no getting away from it.' Then she looked pointedly at the stove clock. 'It's after eight.'

'I've been waiting for you.' Luke leaned back against the counter. 'So...what's your decision?'

Whitney raised a mocking brow. 'The coffee was a sweetener, then, to put me in a cooperative mood?'

'A man's gotta do what he's gotta do.'

'You needn't have bothered,' she said dryly. Retrieving her mug, she held it cupped in front of her, and the steam rose between them. She looked at him through it. 'I'd already decided to go along with your plan.'

'Terrific.' He grinned. 'You won't regret it.'

'But I'll want to see the contract your lawyer writes up, before I make a *final* decision.'

'Sounds reasonable.'

'And if I sell the Merc, then I want equal access to the truck.'

'No problem. Provided business has priority over pleasure.'

'Of course.' She exhaled a sigh. 'But something's still bothering me.'

'I thought we'd covered all the problem areas?'

'I'm not happy about our arrangements for Troy…'

At the sound of his name, the baby gurgled, and banged his fist on the porridge-caked tray. 'Ma…'

'If he and I are going to be spending a lot of time together,' Whitney went on, 'he's going to become attached to me. It's going to be upsetting for him, when we eventually have to say goodbye to each other.'

'Do you have an alternative suggestion?'

'What about his mother?'

Wham! The atmosphere changed as if she'd tossed a grenade at him. His eyes hardened. His face darkened.

Whitney clutched her mug, wishing it was a magic bottle with a genie that could whisk her to some secret place where Luke's stormy gaze couldn't find her.

'That,' he said harshly, 'is not an option.'

'Well.' Whitney adopted a carefree tone in an attempt to gloss over the tension she'd provoked. 'Let's move on then. How about hiring a nanny, someone permanent, who—'

'No.'

'But—'

'If you're not willing to look after Troy, the deal is off. We just sit tight here, the three of us, and wait till the judge decides if the will is valid.'

'But if we do that—'

'Yeah?'

'It'll be too late to graft. At least this year.'

'Right.'

'But that's...such a waste of time. And an unwise move, financially.'

Troy shoved his spoon off the tray and it clattered to the floor. He started to cry.

Luke stared at Whitney. Her eyebrows rose...and when she saw the challenge in his expression, they rose even further.

She met his gaze steadily for a long moment, and then she released a taut breath and put down her mug. Freeing Troy from his high chair, she hoisted him up in her arms.

He stopped crying and plunged his fingers happily into her hair; the shiny clasp, at last, was within his reach!

Whitney held him firmly and directed a level gaze at his father. 'I've never looked after a baby before,' she said. 'What I know about children could be written on the point of a needle.'

Luke's smile transformed his face.

He pushed himself from the counter. 'Then I'll have to give you a crash course. Lesson 1 coming up: The Bath.'

CHAPTER SIX

'WAKEY-WAKEY! Rise and shine...'

Whitney groaned out a protest, and squirreled her way more deeply under her bed covers.

The sound of her curtains being tugged open ran irritatingly along her nerves.

'Stop it.' Her mutter was muffled. 'Go away!'

'I've brought you a mug of coffee.'

Coffee.

She pushed her feet to the bottom of the bed, stuck out her arms and stretched. She peered at her watch, and when she saw it wasn't yet six, croaked a disbelieving 'Ye gods!'

Shoving herself jerkily up on one elbow, she was in time to see Luke loping away toward the door. Her bleary gaze encompassed the white T-shirt pulled taut over his wide shoulders; the narrow-fitting blue jeans that delineated the hard musculature of his legs; and the energy that positively shimmered from him in electrical waves. She shuddered.

'Wait!' Her voice was rusty. 'What's going on here?'

He turned. 'Troy's awake,' he said. 'I've changed him, so he'll play happily in his crib—' his eyes had a malicious glint '—for just about as long as it takes you to drink your coffee and have a quick shower.'

Whitney raked her tumbled hair back from her face, and Luke's gaze dropped to her scantily clad breasts.

Her heart gave a little lurch as she realized her scoop-neck nightie had slid over to one side as she raised her arm, revealing a swell of creamy flesh. Her immediate impulse was to cover herself; she stubbornly resisted. If this man wanted to invade her privacy—even with the best of intentions…she *presumed* with the best of intentions; he didn't *seem* to be the voyeur type—then if he chanced to be confronted by any part of her anatomy that he found distracting that was *his* problem.

'Thanks for the coffee.' She reached over to the bedside table for the mug. 'But I bet you forgot sugar.' She took a tentative sip…and raised her brows. 'Well, hallelujah!'

'Hallelujah indeed.' His gaze was still avidly on her exposed flesh, like glistening blue sequins fixed there with glue. 'Well, I'll be off.' He cleared his throat. Shifted his feet. Looked exceedingly uncomfortable.

Whitney let her own gaze drift down over his tall frame…and saw that his washed-soft baby blue jeans were fitting him more snugly by the moment…

She felt a flush rise to her cheeks, and prayed he wouldn't notice it. As for the spark of amusement dancing in her eyes, she was pretty sure he was too far away to detect that—but then, he wasn't looking at her eyes, was he?

'So…see you later.' She took another sip of her coffee, and watched him over the rim of the mug.

'You won't drop off to sleep again, will you?'

'No—and you needn't worry about Troy. Your

''crash course'' yesterday was pretty intensive. We covered every aspect of his daily routine, and I'm going to manage just fine—*we*'re going to manage just fine, your son and I!'

'You're sure?'

'Absolutely.'

'Okay.' His Adam's apple bobbed up and down. He scraped a hand over his jaw and Whitney heard the rasping sound from across thc room. 'Later, then. I'll leave the door ajar, so you'll be able to listen for the kid.'

And he left. Finally he left, but dragging his feet. All that energy that had been emanating from him…where had it gone!

With a wry smile, Whitney glanced down…and her face froze in a mask of horror. When she'd reached for the mug, her nightie had slipped even further askew, and there for all the world to see, was one perfect rose pink nipple.

Aargh! The strangled sound came from between her lips as she snatched the nightie back into place…but too late.

Far too late.

She grimaced. What must Luke be thinking of her? Brazen. The word popped into her mind, along with a few more, some of them unprintable.

Well, that was nothing new, was it!

Still, she drank down the rest of her coffee in one big gulp, and springing out of bed, hurried to the shower.

* * *

After lunch that day, Luke announced he was going into Penticton. He came home around five, but said not a word over dinner about the purpose or outcome of his trip.

That night, as Whitney was making for the stairs on her way to bed, he emerged from the library.

'Hang on a minute,' he said.

One hand deep in the pocket of her terry robe, the other wrapped around a mug of marshmallow-trimmed hot chocolate, Whitney paused at the foot of the stairs.

'So,' he said, 'how'd the baby-sitting go today?'

'Your son's had me on the trot since dawn, and chose this afternoon to waken early from his nap. I'm not sure which one of us is the more worn out!'

'I was just going through to the kitchen to get myself a beer. Are you too tired to talk?'

'About what?'

'The will.'

'Oh.' Whitney shrugged. 'No, I *am* tired...but it's okay.' She turned and started back toward the kitchen.

Luke was right beside her, and pushed open the door.

She crossed to the table and sat down.

He walked over to the fridge, took out a can of lager, popped the top and took a healthy swallow. A froth clung to his upper lip. Whitney found herself fascinated by it...

Absently he flicked the froth away with the tip of his tongue. 'Marilla Eaton has filed my Writ of Summons and Statement of Claim.'

As she'd watched his tongue, Whitney had felt a

hot little quiver of desire somewhere below the pit of her stomach; nothing could have doused that fire with more speed than his calmly spoken words.

She'd known, of course, that he planned to contest the will; still, she felt rocked by the news that he'd actually set things in motion. She tried to keep her voice as calm as his had been, as she said, 'So what do I have to do?'

'Maxwell will file your Statement of Defence. Then the estate will be frozen, and the court will appoint an administrator—Marilla assures me we should have no problem getting authority from him to operate the vineyard the way we want to in the meantime.'

'And the hearing date?'

'We're looking at least a year down the road.' He dragged his brows down in a bad-tempered frown. 'There'll undoubtedly be a mountain of paper-work…and if the case drags on, do you know who's going to benefit most?'

Whitney's laugh was cynical. 'You, of course, if you win—'

'Our lawyers. Ms. Eaton stands to rake in twenty percent of what I come out of this with if I win, and as for Edmund Maxwell—whichever way it goes, he'll make a bundle.'

'Surely you don't expect them to work for nothing? Lawyers have huge overheads—'

'There's one way you and I can keep the whole kit and caboodle to ourselves.'

'And how could we do that?' Whitney didn't try to keep the skepticism from her voice.

Luke snapped his beer can down on the table, and

put his hands on his hips. 'We could settle out of court.'

Now what devious plan had he come up with? Nothing to *her* advantage, she could be sure! 'I'm listening.'

'It really galls me to pay out good money when we don't have to—'

'But we do have to, don't we? Look, this discussion is a waste of time. It's up to a judge to decide who gets the estate—and since I'm the one holding all the cards, why on earth would I be interested in settling out of court?'

'Whitney—' his mouth was grim '—my case is rock solid.'

'*Case*? Luke, you don't *have* a case. If you think that just because you're a Brannigan and the estate's been in your family for generations, the judge will overturn the will, you'll have to think again. No way would a—'

'Before I went to see my lawyer, I paid a visit to Dr. McKay and he told me something…interesting. A couple of days before my grandmother's accident, apparently you went to his office and asked him to prescribe sleeping pills for her—'

'She was suffering from insomnia.' Why on earth would Luke have found that particularly interesting? 'Wc didn't know then about her tumor, of course, and it may have already been causing her…discomfort. At any rate, when I suggested sleeping pills, she agreed to—'

'So…it was *your* idea?'

There was a slight change in his tone, but Whitney

couldn't interpret it…though she did think it had had an odd sort of 'Ah-*hah*!' edge. Puzzling. 'Yes. But she didn't want to see Dr. McKay—didn't want him ''poking around'' as she put it—so he would only prescribe enough for a couple of weeks.'

'And she took the pills?'

'Mmm.'

'But not all of them, of course…at least, not before her accident, if he gave her enough to last a couple of weeks. So…when she got out of hospital, did she continue taking them? The ones left in the bottle?'

Where on earth was Luke going with this? 'That's a year ago…I really don't remember…she may have…'

'When my grandmother was released from hospital, the surgeon prescribed strong painkillers to be taken at home as needed. Were they needed?'

'Oh, yes.' Whitney felt her heart clench as distressing memories surged up. 'They were needed.'

'Might you have given her the sleeping pills, too, if she'd asked for them…for added comfort?'

'I *really* don't remember. Luke, it was such a traumatic time—'

'She wrote her will a couple of days after she came home from hospital, didn't she?'

Whitney frowned. 'Yes, but—'

'So taking into account that she was getting on in years, it's likely that when she wrote the will, she'd not only have been weak and tired—and at a low ebb, as you've already told me—which would have made her susceptible to suggestion, but if she was taking a mixture of painkillers and sleeping pills she'd have been quite out of it. Not altogether of—'

'*Sound mind*?' Whitney's heartbeats took off at a walloping gallop but they barely kept pace with the fury sweeping through her.

'When I talked it over with Marilla, she said—'

Whitney had surged to her feet. 'Oh, I can guess *exactly* what your lady lawyer said! "Luke, honey, this is fantastic! We'll break your old grannie's will in no time flat. She was senile, poor dear—and not only senile but drugged, a *pushover* for that wicked Whitney McKenzie." Undue influence, isn't it called, Luke?' Eyes blazing, she swept her hair back, her hands shaking. 'My God.' Shock reverberated through her with the power of an earthquake. 'I don't believe it—is *that* the basis for your claim?'

'Yes.' His voice was steady. 'That is the basis for my claim.'

Pounding pulses sledgehammered Whitney's temples. 'But just in case a judge might not be convinced, you're blackmailing me now—threatening to drag my name through the mud, because you believe that to avoid having that happen, I'll surrender and go under without a fight—'

'Now, hang on a minute. All I'm saying is that rather than have the lawyers make a killing, you and I can sort this thing out between ourselves. I want this estate and I mean to have it...it's my birthright. But I'm prepared to offer you a settlement—ten percent of what the vineyard is worth—'

'*Forget it*!' Rage was a red blur in her eyes. Oh, she wasn't fighting him over the estate—at least, not because of its monetary value; she would have fought just as hard over something worth only a dollar. She was fighting him because she despised his tactics…and because right was on her side. 'Your grandmother wanted *me* to have this place—this whole place, not ten percent of it, nor twenty percent of it, not thirty percent of it! One hundred percent of it, Luke—and nothing you—or your precious lady lawyer—can do will ever change that fact!'

Luke lurched to his feet and towered over her like a wrathful giant. 'And nothing will ever change the fact that your mother destroyed my family, and if she hadn't, neither of us would be in this damnable situation now!' His hands were clenched into fists and Whitney sensed that if she'd been a man, she'd already be lying splattered on the carpet. 'She seduced my father and was responsible for my mother's suicide—and ultimately she was responsible for my father's death. If she hadn't been hell-bent on skiing that day, he wouldn't have been killed in that avalanche—'

'My mother died in that avalanche, too, Luke, and that's why your grandmother gave me a home.' Whitney's face felt as white as the snow that had buried Ben and her mother. 'And you just can't forgive that, can you, Luke! You can't ever forgive your grandmother for giving a home to the child of the woman you hated. Oh, I can still remember your face that first day we met—if I'd ever seen murder in anyone's eyes, it was in yours.'

Wearily, drained of her anger, she shook her head. 'I'm not my mother, Luke. Nor have I ever been…or ever will be...responsible for her actions. And till you can see that,' she concluded as she turned away, 'then you and I will never be able to settle *anything* between us...

'Either in court, or out of it.'

Next day, interaction between them was chillingly distant, except when Troy was within hearing distance, at which times, by unspoken agreement, they both kept up a facade of normalcy.

Under the surface of that normalcy, however, surged a violent sea of emotion, and when Whitney was in Luke's presence, she felt unbearably aware of him. Despite their mutual hostility, his sexual magnetism continued to pull at her as inexorably as a hook pulling a helpless fish.

She sometimes wondered, with a feeling of mingled dread and despair, how she'd resist, if he ever tried to land her.

The following day, Luke told her, curtly, that he'd found a buyer in Penticton for the Mercedes. After the necessary paperwork was completed, she accepted Luke's offer to deliver the vehicle to its new owner.

When he returned, he was driving a small red Honda.

'For you,' he said. 'You need your own set of wheels. I won't always be able to let you have the truck—I'll need to have it handy for driving over to the Sagebrush Vineyards on a daily basis to pick up fresh cuttings—and you and Troy can't be stuck up here all summer long. The car's twelve years old and has over 100,000 kilometers on the clock, but it's immaculate inside and runs like a sewing machine.'

'Can we afford it?' Whitney asked stiffly.

He held out the key, in the palm of his hand.

Whitney looked at it. It was only a key, wasn't it? Yet, there was a stillness about Luke, a feeling of…waiting. And all at once she sensed it wasn't just the key he was offering her. It was also an olive branch.

'Thanks,' she said quietly as she accepted it. 'And Luke—'

'Yeah?'

'Let's forget about kitchen rotas and suchlike. Since you're going to be out working in the fields all day, I'll take over the cooking.'

'Fair enough—'

She cleared her throat. 'But in the evenings—'

'"You in your small parlor, and I in mine"?' His smile was dry. 'Sure, no problem.'

She recognized his quote but couldn't place it. Was it from an old nursery rhyme? A song? It didn't matter. What did matter was Luke's easy acceptance of the line she'd just drawn between their working hours and their leisure hours.

After his accusation that she'd used 'undue influence' on his grandmother, the last thing she wanted to do was spend her free time in his company. Their relationship was a business one, and that was the way she wanted to keep it.

For the next few weeks, Whitney saw little of Luke.

He was up and out of the house every morning by

five-thirty. Spraying for weeds had to be done at that early hour, she knew, because the air was calm then, with no breeze that might drift poison up to the vines.

The team of grafters from California arrived on schedule, and parked their campers down by the lake. They worked overtime with a team of local workers to lop off the existing vines at knee height and remove loose bark, prior to grafting the cuttings onto the existing hybrid roots.

Luke did some grafting, too, but his work was not limited to doing that and supervising the grafting crews. Whitney knew he was responsible for obtaining good cuttings, and then ensuring they were properly labeled and stored in damp sawdust and wrapped in plastic so they wouldn't dry out. He also kept the crews supplied with grafting tape and paint; checked to make sure their grafting knives were kept extremely sharp; used the narrow vineyard tractor to cut the grass between the vine rows...and performed endless other tasks, the multiplicity of which made Whitney's job of looking after Troy seem a sinecure by comparison!

May brought warmer weather...and June brought flowers to the vines.

It also brought long hazy days and sensual summer nights. And if Whitney ever felt a strange restlessness as she lay in bed she tried not to think about it...or about the man sleeping in the next room.

Instead she focused her thoughts, and her energies, on his son.

Troy was thriving, and hardly a day passed that he didn't do something new to delight her. Though he hadn't started walking yet, by late June he'd managed the odd wavering step, and she knew he'd soon be taking off under his own steam.

One afternoon, after wheeling him around the garden in his stroller, she set him down on the lawn, and rolled his large multicolored ball away along the grass.

'There,' she said encouragingly, 'go get it!'

With a squeal, Troy tottered off in its wake, obviously forgetting his unsteadiness as he focused on the big ball. He managed eight or nine steps on his own, before he stumbled and fell flat. Chuckling, he reached out for the ball, which had rolled to a halt in front of him.

'Clever boy!' Whitney cried, and scooted over to help him to his feet. She pushed the ball away again, and he took off again after it. With a merry laugh, she watched him.

'I'm glad I saw that.' Luke's quiet voice came from behind her.

She whirled around. 'Luke! I didn't hear you—'

'I didn't want to distract Troy.'

Maybe he should have worried more about distracting *her*, Whitney thought as she tried to steady her suddenly jolting heartbeats. His face was shadowed by the wide brim of his battered straw hat, but she could still see the glint of sexual awareness in his eyes as he looked at her. It set sparks of excitement, like a series of tiny fireworks, exploding from nerve to nerve throughout her body.

Fortunately Troy had spotted his father, and his

gleeful shriek as he scrambled crabwise toward him broke the moment of tension.

'Hey, kid, how's it going?' Luke hoisted the child up on his shoulders. 'Walking by yourself already, huh? Pretty soon you're going to be working in the vineyards with me. I wish,' Luke addressed Whitney, 'that I'd had a video camera there, so I could have—'

'Captured the moment. I know, it's something very special, seeing a baby take his very first steps.'

'Not only Troy. You. The two of you together.'

Oh, Lord, she thought, don't keep looking at me like that. You'll have me throwing myself at your feet, begging you to have your wicked way with me.

'Well, thank you,' she said, awkwardly. 'Now…if you'll excuse us, I was about to take Troy for a splash in the pool before I put him down for his nap.' She hesitated. 'What are you doing home at this time? You don't usually—'

'I need to make a couple of phone calls.' He squinted up against the sun, and she saw sweat running down his brow. 'But I must say, a dip sounds good. I'll make my calls.' He transferred Troy to Whitney's arms. 'And then I'll see you both in the water.'

He took off, his long stride eating up the space between the lawn and the front door of the house.

'Oh, Lord.' Whitney screwed up her nose as she watched him depart. Luke had been too busy to open up the pool until just a couple of weeks ago, and since then, she'd always timed Troy's water play and her own swimming sessions, for occasions when Luke wasn't around. Still…to opt out would surely make him wonder if she felt vulnerable around him. She was...but she didn't want *him* to know that!

Sighing, she strapped Troy into his stroller and as she did, heard the sound of a vehicle chugging up the hill. She glanced round, and saw Hetty's old pink Cadillac pulling up in the forecourt. The brunette emerged a moment later, her plump figure clad in a floral sundress.

She crossed the lawn, her cheery 'Hi, there, Miss McKenzie!' preceding her. After fussing over Troy, she said, 'Is Luke around, honey?'

'He just went inside. If you'll watch Troy for a minute, I'll go in and—'

'Oh, don't bother.' Hetty took a magazine out of her capacious handbag and gave it to Whitney. 'He might like to see this—maybe he already has, but then maybe he hasn't.'

Whitney glanced at the magazine, a glossy called *Napa Valley Illustrated.* 'Sure, I'll give it to him. Won't you come in, and have a glass of something cold?'

'Thanks anyway.' Hetty's beehive hairdo quivered as she shook her head. 'But I've gotta get back—my sister's here on holiday. She's from Los Angeles and she always saves up her magazines for me to put in the salon. This one—' she nodded toward the glossy in Whitney's hand '—is from this Spring. There's a picture of Luke's spread, page 94. Well, I've really gotta go. Nice to see you again, though.'

'You, too.' Whitney's voice echoed in her head, as if it came from outer space. *Luke's spread*?

She was barely aware of the Cadillac's tires spitting

up gravel as Hetty took off again. Fingers fumbling, she turned over the pages, till she came to page 94.

Her gaze veered first to the two photographs. Vividly colored photographs. One was of a gorgeous red-roofed house, Mediterranean-style. The other was an aerial picture of a vineyard whose acreage looked to be around half that of the Emerald Valley Vineyard.

Confusion dulled Whitney's mind. Hetty must be wrong; this couldn't belong to Luke. He'd told her he had no money; and no assets.

Below the photos, was a short article.

She read the heading, uneasiness growing inside her, along with a prickling feeling of apprehension: Paradise For Sale.

. Frowning, she continued to read:

> Luke Brannigan's Mountain Paradise Vineyard went on the market last month, and was immediately purchased by Rafe Marconi and his wife Jude, who own the neighboring Blue Hills Winery. 'To say we are thrilled,' Jude enthused after the deal had gone through, 'is an understatement. Mountain Paradise is a gem. It has exceptional grapes and we've always been interested in running an organic vineyard. The price, of course, was steep…but we know this is the very best investment we could make with our money…'

The magazine slipped from Whitney's fingers and fell with a rustle to the ground. Dazedly she bent to pick it up…and suddenly became aware that Troy was grumbling.

How long had she been standing there, staring disbelievingly at the page?

The sun was still blazing down. But her heart felt cold. Her whole body felt cold. Chilled.

He had lied to her.

And he had really fooled her.

Not only had he fooled her, but he had also somehow managed to involve his lawyer and his banker in the deception.

Yet something in her balked at that. Surely no lawyer, no banker, would go along with that kind of cover-up; no matter the reason. He must have lied to them, too.

And as that realization hit her, the chilled feeling that was paralyzing her began to be replaced by anger. Anger that blazed up inside her with such intensity she wanted to scream, as if by doing so she could vent her feelings of fury and outrage…and contempt.

'Ma-ma-ma…' Troy's voice—whimpery, as if he'd sensed her distress—made her refocus her thoughts.

Tight-lipped, she rolled up the magazine and rammed it into the stroller's carrier bag. Hetty had wanted her to give it to Luke? Oh, she'd give it to him all right….

She could hardly wait.

CHAPTER SEVEN

LUKE was already in the water when she wheeled Troy around the back of the house to the pool.

He was swimming laps, and didn't notice their arrival till after Whitney had stripped Troy and put on his swim trunks. She was just about to sit him in the stroller till she got herself ready, when Luke saw them.

He crossed to the shallow end and stood there with the sun gilding his sparkling wet body.

'Here.' He reached up. 'I'll take him till you get changed.'

As she transferred the baby to his care, Luke's hands brushed her fingers. The touch sent a tingle of sensation up her arms; before Hetty's visit, with its implications, that touch might have excited her, now it only repulsed her.

'Thanks,' she said, her tone purposely casual, and turned away.

She was wearing her swimsuit under her shorts and shirt. The bikini was black. The fabric silk. The cut subtle…

The effect, she knew, anything but.

Before Hetty's visit, she'd have gone over to the gazebo to undress, reluctant to take off her clothes in front of Luke even though she had on a swimsuit under them.

Now she had no such inhibitions.

On the contrary, it would give her a certain grim pleasure to deliberately reveal herself to him. She already knew he found her desirable. To arouse him by performing a striptease would be…in a coldly clinical way…a rather interesting maneuver.

She sauntered along the pool's ceramic-tiled apron toward the diving board at the far end. When she got there, she lazily toed off her sandals, appearing to be giving only a vague part of her attention to Luke, who was now playing with Troy. He was holding the squealing child just above the waist, sweeping him teasingly in, again and again, an inch or so farther each time.

He glanced her way and called over, 'He's a champ—definitely has Olympic possibilities.' His grin was infectious.

Or at least she would have found it so, had it come her way before the pink Cadillac had chugged up the driveway…

Whitney gave him a fake smile in return.

And raking her fingers through her hair, spread it out provocatively over her shoulders. The seductive gesture of vamp…and she saw it wasn't lost on Luke. His brows rose, very faintly…but unmistakably.

Whitney felt the first small surge of smug elation.

Her shorts had an elasticised waistband. She could have slipped them off in two seconds flat. She turned sideways, so her profile was to the pool; she could no longer see Luke, but she knew with every breath she took that he was watching. She counted twenty-three beats of her heart—including the time it took to fold the garment loosely—before she dropped it on the blue and gold tiles.

Luke was still splashing Troy in and out of the water, but not so quickly now, and more irregularly.

Her shirt had five buttons. She opened the first, and stepped onto the diving board. Opened the second, walked slowly forward. Opened the third, and the fourth.

And let her glance move, with frank innocence, to Luke.

He was still dipping Troy into the water, but slowly, his movements almost at a standstill…and he was paying scant attention to what he was doing.

Whitney got to the end of the diving board, and threw him an open smile. And then lifted her shoulders, rotated them slightly, as if to ease a slight tension there.

'Mmm.' Her voice came out huskily. 'What a gorgeous day…'

Closing her eyes, she opened the fifth button, let her head fall back. Shrugging off the shirt, she let it fall behind her to the board. Her hair moved with a silky slither over the smooth skin of her back. The sun moved with a sensuous caress over the naked swell of her breasts.

She could feel Luke's eyes on her. It made her shiver, as if he had scraped a fingernail down her spine.

She straightened, bounced the board gently, raised her arms in preparation for her dive.

And at the very last moment, she allowed her glance to skip back to Luke.

His gaze was dark, his expression spellbound. His lips were tight; his body taut.

Her dive was perfect.

She surfaced right in front of him—so close to him she could see the flicker of a nerve in his cheek.

Panting a little, she smoothed back her sodden hair and then spent a moment unnecessarily adjusting her bikini top, letting her breasts bounce a little as she tugged the spaghetti straps in place.

'You call that a swimsuit?' Luke's voice was hoarse. 'I've seen stamps that were bigger.'

She gave a throaty laugh. 'You don't like it?'

'I didn't say that—'

'Out!' Troy wriggled frustratedly in his father's arms. 'Out!'

'Had enough, little fella?' Whitney took the chubby hand thrust out at her. 'I think,' she said, flirting with Luke with her eyes, 'that he's ready for bed.'

'He's not the only one.'

She pasted an amused smile on her face. 'Why don't you take him up then…and go for a nap, too?'

He couldn't keep his eyes off her. She knew how revealing her bikini top was. How very tantalizing it must be for him to see so much…and to think of what was concealed by the scrap of black silk. So near… and yet so far. Only…he had no idea just how far!

And here, in the pool, Troy was her protection. As long as he was in Luke's arms, she was safe.

She ran the fingertips of one hand over Luke's forearm, that sexy forearm sprinkled with wet gold.

'Off you go,' she murmured. 'I'm going to swim a few laps before I come up.'

His eyes had an odd glazed look, as if his thoughts had leaped forward. He cleared his throat. 'See you then.'

'Sure.'

She watched as he waded away toward the ladder, with Troy's arms wound tightly around his neck. She watched his muscles ripple as he climbed up to the deck. Kept watching as he walked to the patio doors. And found herself—despite her contempt for him—lost in total awe over the sheer beauty of his body, revealed to her in all its masculine glory by a pair of sinfully brief navy trunks.

What a pity that such a magnificent exterior should shelter such a rotten core.

She stood motionless till after he'd slid the patio door shut behind him. And then her legs suddenly collapsed under her. Weakly she let herself fall back into the water, and floated, moving her arms and feet with the minimum amount of energy necessary to keep herself from sinking.

She wasn't cut out to play the role of vamp, but her attempt had been successful. Luke had been aroused. Oh, yes, he had been aroused. He'd commented on the brevity of her bikini…well, he'd had no room to criticize.

She grimaced. None whatever!

The cut of *his* trunks had left little to the imagination.

But what she had to say to him would shrivel his passion as surely as if she'd sluiced him with Arctic water.

* * *

The house was quiet.

As she ran with soft steps up the stairs, she didn't hear a sound. Luke's bedroom door was closed, and she passed it quickly.

Once in her own room, she took some clean undies from her dresser and hurried to the bathroom. For this upcoming confrontation, she wanted to look her best. She'd wear the sage green dress she'd bought two summers ago at Holt Renfrew; it had cost the earth but when she wore it she always felt a surge of self-confidence.

She showered, blow-dried her hair and brushed it till it shone with the rich red of a November sunset. Then she slipped on her lacy bra and underpants, before spritzing Gucci's *Accenti* at her pulse points. Her eyes, she noticed as she glanced in the mirror, glittered as if the emerald depths were scattered with crystal, and her lips looked fuller than usual, giving her a sultry expression.

Astonishing, because she didn't feel sultry. What she felt was mad. Mad enough to throw Cressida's antique china plates against a wall and not give a damn about the cost!

She opened the bathroom door and padded, barefoot, into her bedroom—

'At last…'

She stopped short, her eyes wide with disbelief. There, over by her bed, stood Luke, with a grin on his face. He was wearing nothing but a pair of old jeans—zipped, thank heaven…but with the metal button at the waist unsnapped, so the edges of the waistband hung open.

'Luke.' Somehow she managed to regain her aplomb...on the surface, at least. '*Quelle surprise*!' she added lightly.

'Surely not.' He moved toward her. 'Your invitation was—'

She slipped out of reach and made for her closet. 'I don't recall having issued any invitation.' She opened the closet door and reached for the sage green dress.

His hand circled her wrist before she got to the hanger. 'Don't play games,' he said. 'You're not a child, Whitney. Your seductive little striptease out there was a turn-on...as you planned it to be.'

She tugged her wrist free and stepped back. 'You invited yourself to join us at the pool. Did you expect me to leave my clothes on and dive in with my—'

'There are ways and ways of taking your clothes off.' His lips had become hard-looking. 'And you—'

'I made you want me. Is that what you're trying to say?'

'That's exactly what I'm saying.' His hands were all at once on her shoulders, pulling her toward him till they were so close his breath winnowed over her parted lips.

She swallowed. Kept her body stiff.

'Let me go,' she said. 'I have something to say to you before we go any further.'

For a moment he didn't yield, and her heart gave an anxious lurch; then he released her. Going over to the closed door, he leaned back against it, barring her way out.

She turned her back on him, and reached for the

sage green dress. She slipped it on quickly and did up the front buttons—but for once the expensive designer outfit didn't work its usual magic; she felt drained of confidence. And apprehension spilled in to fill the resulting vacuum.

She turned.

'Well?' Luke's tone was quiet.

She wished the dress had pockets, so she could slip her hands into them. She twined her fingers together, then realizing she might be revealing her nervousness she untwined them again. She walked over to the dresser, and picked up Hetty's magazine. She ran her thumb pads over it for a moment, before raising her eyes and meeting Luke's.

'I want you to leave,' she said.

'You said you wanted to talk—'

'I don't mean just leave this room. I mean...I want you to leave this house. Today.'

He stared at her. 'I don't underst—'

'How long did you think you could get away with this, Luke? How long before I found out you were lying?'

'Lying?' He pushed himself abruptly from the door, and strode toward her, his brows lowered in a ferocious glower. 'What the hell are you talking about?'

Whitney cringed inside, but stood her ground.

She tilted back her head and met his angry gaze. 'The game's up. Hetty was here while you were making your phone calls.' She thrust the magazine at him. 'She gave me this. For you.'

He took it; riffled the pages. 'What am I supposed to be looking for?'

'Page 94.'

Frowning, he turned the pages. She didn't look at the magazine; she looked at his face, and she knew the moment he reached page 94. His features froze. It was apparent he'd never seen the article before.

Silence hummed in the room while he read it.

It didn't take him long.

When he looked at her again, his blue eyes had become a wintry gray.

'You've read it,' he said. 'And you've come to your own conclusions.'

'You're a liar, Luke. You have no right to be here, staying in this house. I wonder how you can live with yourself, under the circumstances—'

'The circumstances?' His voice was even colder than the expression in his eyes. 'And what have you, with your limited knowledge, decided those circumstances are?'

'You're not penniless. Far from it.' She swept her hand contemptuously over the magazine. 'You've more money than you know what to do with. You're here under false pretenses. You're devious and dishonest. I despise you.' She started to turn away. 'I never want to see you aga—'

The sound of the magazine being smashed onto the dresser made her jump. The grasp of his hand on her shoulder made her yelp.

'Let me go!' She spun away from him, rounded the bed and glared at him with the space of it between them. 'Don't you ever lay a finger on me, you…you cheat, you liar, you—'

She gave a little shriek of alarm as he bounded over the bed and grabbed her again.

His fingers dug into her upper arms. 'Cut it out!' he gritted. 'Stop that shouting, you're going to waken Troy—'

'You told me you had no money!' She spat the words up at him.

'I don't *have* any money!'

'I don't believe you! You couldn't possibly have spent what you got for your property between the time you sold it and the time you turned up here. And even if you *had* spent it, you should have something to show for it, dammit! What did you buy, Luke—what did you just *have* to have,' she jeered, 'that was so necessary to you, so very *special* that it left you without a penny in the bank?'

With a suddenness that stunned her, he released her. It was almost as if...as if she'd slapped him. Or punched him, without warning, in the stomach. His face had paled, his features had become grim. He moved away from her, crossed to the window and stood there with his back to her.

'Luke—' Whitney's voice faltered '—Luke, did I...say something I...?'

He didn't answer, but the tension in the air was unlike any that had existed between them before.

Shakily she got to her feet. 'What is it, Luke? Please tell me...'

After a long, long silence, he finally spoke.

'I did spend all my money.' His voice came over his shoulder, muffled. 'On something...very special to me.'

'I...don't understand.'

He put a hand against the edge of the window frame, stiffly, as if to support himself. 'I divorced my wife this spring. I had to sell everything I owned, in order to give her the settlement she demanded.'

'Settlement?' Whitney wished he would turn, because it was difficult talking to him when she couldn't read his expression. 'But surely...wouldn't you each get half? Isn't that how property settlements work, these days, when a marriage breaks up?'

'Not when the wife wants a...different deal.'

Whitney took a few steps toward him. 'What kind of a deal?'

'She wanted money.' His tone was weary. 'I wanted Troy.'

'Are you saying...she didn't?' But even as disbelief coursed through her, Dixie's words drifted into her mind: That poor little kid, he's had a helluva start to his life so far.

Luke's answer didn't come in words; it lay in the rigidity of his muscles. Whitney felt goose bumps rise on her skin.

'Dear God,' she whispered, 'why didn't you tell me?'

At last he turned...and when she saw the haunted expression in his eyes, she almost wished he hadn't.

'Would you want anyone to know,' he asked, 'that you'd had to buy your own child?'

Whitney closed the short distance between them in the space of a heartbeat and took Luke's hands in hers.

'Oh, Luke.' Compassion made her voice soft. 'I had

no idea…' Tears blurred her vision as she looked up at him. 'Please forgive me for what I said—'

'I may be many things, Whitney. A liar isn't one of them.'

'I know.' The words trembled. 'I'm so sorry. I just wish—'

'What?'

'That I could take back what I said. I should've asked you about the article, instead of jumping to conclusions.'

'I guess I shouldn't have flown off the handle the way I did…'

She sensed that was about as close to an apology as she was going to get. And suddenly she realized she was still clasping his hands. She dropped them, and rather awkwardly grasped her elbows instead. 'I'm glad Hetty brought you the magazine,' she said. 'It helps me…understand you.'

His mouth slanted in a self-derisive smile. 'What's to understand? I'm just a simple guy…'

His tone had been light, and Whitney kept hers equally light as she retorted, 'That's debatable!'

But now that the level of emotion had lowered slightly, she became aware of a different kind of tension dragging between them. And intensely aware of his naked chest just inches away.

Flight was definitely called for…

'Well,' she said, 'I'm glad at least that we've cleared the air.' With what she hoped looked like a casual smile, she turned away from him and crossed to the door. 'And now that we've settled everything…' She curved her fingers around the doorknob...only to find a large hand clamping itself on top of hers.

'Not quite everything.' His voice was husky. 'We still have some...unfinished business.'

The dark intent in his eyes set her heartbeats into overdrive. Weakly she fell back against the wall. 'We do?' Her voice came out faintly. 'I don't think—'

'Good,' he said. 'I don't want you to think.' And as she parted her lips to protest, his mouth zeroed in on hers with an arrogant male self-assurance that jellied her knees.

His kiss was sensual and passionate; his hands inescapable as he swung hers out and pressed them to the wall at shoulder level, either side of her. His body leaning against hers was arrogant, and moved in a subtle yet seductive way that fired her blood.

She inhaled a quivering breath—and from his hair drew in the lingering smell of chlorine, from his hands that sweet scent of baby talc. His lips slid from hers, to nuzzle the skin below her ear where she had spritzed her perfume.

'Mmm,' he murmured, 'you smell good. Good enough to eat...'

With a moan, she arched her head back...and obviously taking that as an invitation, Luke skimmed his lips to her throat, caressing the pale smooth skin, tracing a path down, over her collarbone, to the low neckline of her dress...

Only then did he release her hands. And without lessening the pressure of his lower body, he started undoing the buttons—just as slowly, just as deliberately, as she'd unbuttoned her shirt earlier, while she'd walked along the diving board.

Her hands were now free; she could have pushed him away. But as his body moved sinuously against hers, she let them fall helplessly, limply, to her side.

'Don't.' Her voice was languourous, totally lacking conviction. 'Don't do that. You mustn't...'

He opened the last button, the one just above her waist. And parted the dress.

She closed her eyes, let her head fall back even further. Surrendered to sensation.

He cupped her breasts, tenderly, as if they were the most fragile things he'd ever touched. He held them, in his palms, for several long moments, the way he would hold something infinitely to be treasured. Then she felt him fumble with the bra's front clasp, and she knew, without looking, that his gaze was fixed, cloudily, on his task.

She heard the faint sound as he undid the snaps, and felt her breasts tumble from their confinement. His breath whispered over the rounded swell of flesh, and over the hard bud that just a short time before had been as soft as silk.

'Beautiful.' His voice had a raspy edge. 'Oh, so beautiful...'

His lips closed over one aching tip. She gasped as invisible silver threads tugged every nerve ending, sending electrical tingles sizzling through her. She had the odd sensation that she was floating...and was aware of no worldly thing other than his lips on her flesh. Caressing. His tongue on the tip. Flicking.

Tantalizing. Erotic. Pleasure so exquisite, so intense, it was akin to pain.

And she wanted it never to end.

'Don't stop,' she whispered. 'Oh, please don't—'

Troy's scream shrilled through her pleas.

Whitney froze; Luke's lips were still at her breast, she could feel the warm moistness of them on her skin. She could also feel the raised imprint of his body against her own, and the hard thud of his pulse.

'Damn!' His oath was so quietly muttered she almost missed it. He raised his head, their eyes met; his were glassy, unfocused. He groaned. Then kissed her full on the lips, a lingering kiss…ran his palms possessively, over her breasts, before gently gathering the dress back around her.

Her breathing was labored…her cheeks on fire. She watched, heart thudding out of control, as he left the room.

Her legs were wobbling under her. With fingers shaking, she fastened her bra, and the buttons of her dress.

What a remarkable escape.

She couldn't believe what she had so nearly done. If Troy's cry hadn't broken the spell—

A shudder raked through her. Bad enough that she'd let Luke go as far as he had; she didn't know how she was going to face him again.

She slipped on her sandals and went back into the bathroom. She tidied her hair, powdered her flushed cheeks and carefully applied a coat of peach lipstick. And after checking to make sure every button of her dress was securely in place, she ventured out into the corridor.

She had to pass Troy's room to get to the stairs.

Steps cushioned and soundless on the hallway carpet, she paused when she came to the open doorway.

Luke was leaning over the crib, murmuring soothing words. Troy was whimpering, but even as she listened, the whimpering faded, and she soon heard the steady breathing that told her he'd dropped off to sleep. Luke arranged the bedclothes loosely over the small figure, and then straightened. For a long time, he stood looking down at his sleeping son, his expression gentle and filled with love.

The sight made Whitney's heart ache; filled her with a yearning so intense it hurt. A small sound came from her throat...

Luke turned, and when he saw her, his features tensed. She stepped back into the corridor as he came to join her.

Very quietly he closed the door behind him.

'He must have had a bad dream,' he murmured.

'Mmm.'

They stood there, the tension between them coiled even tighter than it had been earlier. Whitney felt it sizzle in the air...and in her blood.

His smoky gaze ran over her tidied hair, her lipsticked mouth. 'You're...going downstairs?'

The desire in his eyes sucked all the energy from her limbs. She wanted to lean back against the wall...but somehow managed to remain upright. 'I think that would be...wise.'

'Wise?' He looped his arms around her. 'Who

wants to be wise?' The words were almost lost to her, amid the loud clamor of her heartbeats.

'Sex without...love...it's just not for me.'

'You think it's wrong?'

'I don't judge anyone else, but for me...for us...it's just...not right.'

'What's so special about us?' He tried to pull her closer, but she resisted.

'Sex without love...is one thing. But sex where one person hates...that's...ugly.'

She knew she'd hit her mark. Would have known it by the dulling of his gaze, even though he hadn't slackened his grip. 'Hates?' He shook his head. 'Maybe I did hate you once, but it was a transferred hate. I don't hate you, Whitney. I—'

'But when you look at me, you still see my mother.'

She saw the flicker of his eyelids. 'I've already told you I'm not a liar, so I won't lie about that. Yes, when I look at you, I see your mother. How could I not?'

How indeed! She knew only too well that in looks, she and her mother were almost identical.

'You see the woman who broke up your parents' marriage.' Her tone was flat.

He dropped his hands, releasing her. 'I won't deny that.'

'Nobody can break up a marriage that isn't already in trouble.'

'That doesn't excuse—'

'Doesn't excuse...but...explains. Or helps to explain. Makes it easier, perhaps, to...forgive. If you never forgive, Luke, it's only yourself you're hurting.

You can't hurt your father anymore...he's beyond your reach now.'

'Are you saying I did hurt my father?'

'When you turned down his invitation to come and live with him—with us—after your mother died...yes, you hurt him deeply.'

'Surely he didn't expect—'

'He hoped.'

'God!' Luke smashed a fist against the wall. 'Will there never be an end to this?' His expression was haggard.

'There will,' Whitney said quietly, 'when you're ready to put it to rest.'

She stepped away from him, and he didn't try to stop her.

CHAPTER EIGHT

THAT NIGHT—because it was a Sunday, and the one evening of the week that Luke didn't go back out to work after dinner—Whitney prepared a special meal.

When he came in from the fields, she was coming downstairs after putting Troy to bed, and as he stood aside to let her by, she was shocked at the bleak look in his eyes. Had he spent the afternoon thinking about what she'd told him about his father? He *had* hurt his father...but was that something she should have kept to herself?

Feeling troubled and guilty, she decided to set the table in the dining room rather then the kitchen. Perhaps the pleasant surroundings would help lighten Luke's mood.

She was setting a bottle of chilled white wine on the table when he came back downstairs after his shower. She heard him cross the front hall and make for the kitchen.

From the dining room, she called, 'In here.'

The sound of his footsteps broke, and then resumed.

When he came in, she was standing behind her chair at one end of the polished mahogany table, her hands resting lightly on the chair back.

Luke had changed into clean jeans and a neatly pressed indigo shirt. His gaze skimmed the elegant room with its taupe walls, glossy white trim, cream and taupe curtains, before settling on the beautifully set table.

He raised his brows. 'What's the occasion?'

'Nothing special. I just thought you might enjoy a meal out of sight of the sink for a change!'

'I don't think I've been in here since I came back home...but it holds many memories!' He crossed toward her. 'It was in this room that my grandmother drummed table manners into me...and rule number one was "Always seat the ladies first."'

Whitney stepped aside to allow him to pull back her chair. The scent of his aftershave came to her, along with the clean fragrance of soap. And the male scent that was distinctively his own. A disturbing mixture.

'Thank you.' She thought he touched her shoulder lightly after he pushed in her chair, but couldn't be sure.

She'd prepared a fresh green salad for starters, followed by a spicy chicken casserole, which she served with asparagus spears, carrots and brown rice.

Luke made no comments regarding the meal till they were drinking their coffee.

'So...my grandmother taught you to cook,' he said. 'And you were an apt pupil.'

'That's a compliment...I guess! But how did you know Cressida was my teacher?'

'When I was a small child, we didn't have a cook here at Brannigan House because my grandmother loved to be in the kitchen. She did all the cooking…and that chicken casserole, as I recall, was a recipe of her own creation.'

'But didn't your mother…I'd have expected she'd have been the one to—'

'Oh.' He shrugged. 'She hated housework. She was into art, music, needlework…that sort of thing… whereas my grandmother was the more practical type, and always on the go—a positive whirlwind of energy, and with such a zest for living—' He broke off and then his tone became gruff. 'At least that's the way I remember her.'

'Keep those memories, Luke, they were the best. But even at the end, she was amazing. She clung to life with such stubbornness, despite the pain she was in.'

She could have bitten her tongue when she saw the flicker of remorse in Luke's eyes. She sensed he deeply regretted not having come back to Brannigan House sooner. He and his grandmother might not have made their peace with each other, but at least they'd have connected again. Now, it was forever too late.

Quickly Whitney set the conversation off in a different direction.

'Did you go right to California, when you left the valley?'

Luke seemed pleased enough to change the subject. 'No, I headed for Vancouver—driving the black BMW my grandmother gave me when I turned seventeen. I knew Ramon—an older buddy who'd moved there from the valley—would put me up.'

'Did you have any money?'

'Some…but I got in with a fast crowd, and it

wasn't going to last long. Ramon threatened to kick me out, and that forced me to take a long, hard look at my situation.'

'What did you do then?'

'I got that kitchen job I told you about, in the Hotel Vancouver. And I sold my car—'

'Ouch!'

'Yeah.' Self-mockery glinted in his eyes. 'Ouch. But I got a hefty amount for it and used some for a down payment on a condo. Eventually I took a bartending course, and switched to working in the hotel lounge. I became friendly with a bunch of the regulars—one of them was a successful stockbroker, who got me interested in the stock market. He encouraged me to start investing…and seven years later, with his help and more than my fair share of luck, I had a pretty healthy bank account. The housing market was at an all-time high, so I sold the condo and made a tidy profit. At that point I was all set to come back to the valley, buy a small vineyard and "show my grandmother." Childish, huh? But fate, in the shape of one Felicia Orrin, got in the way.'

'Felicia Orrin?'

'My wife. I met her my very last shift on the job.' Luke shook his head, as if he still couldn't get over the irony of it. 'She'd come into the bar alone—a girlfriend had stood her up. She was in a chatty mood—'

'And very attractive?' What woman wouldn't have asked that question, Whitney told herself defensively.

'Dark and glossy and expensive-looking—like top-quality bitter chocolate. At any rate, the timing of our meeting was spot on—a chapter of my life was closing, another was about to open…and it was all so damned exciting. I was high on life and *ready* for a night on the town. She'd flown up from California and was due to go back next morning.' He shoved aside his cup and saucer. 'To cut a long story short, when her plane took off, I was on it.'

'Did she have a job?'

'Her uncle Xavier had a vineyard in Napa Valley. She worked—and I use the term loosely—as a secretary in his office. Xavier was a nice guy…and he took a shine to me. Offered me a job for as long as I wanted it.'

'His niece had obviously taken a shine to you, too!'

'Felicia had marriage on her mind. At first I wasn't interested in settling in California, but the longer I stayed away from the valley, the more distant it seemed. My grandmother—my only living relative—had betrayed me, and I decided starting another family—one I could depend on—might not be a bad idea. So…Felicia and I got married and I bought Mountain Paradise.'

'How long ago was that?'

'Close to five years ago now.'

'You…put off having children?'

Abruptly Luke pushed back his chair and got to his feet. 'Let's get these dishes cleared up.'

Whitney stifled a vexed exclamation. She'd obviously touched a raw spot, and he was backing off. Door closed. Well, it was her own fault; she'd had no right to ask such an intimate question.

Wordlessly they carried everything through to the

kitchen. Then as she was slotting the dishes into the dishwasher, Luke said, 'I'm off through to the library. I have a bit of paperwork to catch up on.'

'Fine,' she said, without looking around.

And in a moment, she was alone.

She stayed up later than usual that evening, catching up on some neglected chores, including a huge pile of ironing that she just hadn't gotten around to because Troy kept her so busy during the day.

By the time she'd finished, darkness was falling. She knew she ought to go to bed, or she'd find it hard to get up in the morning...but even though she was tired, she was sure she wouldn't sleep. Not yet. The abrupt end of her dinner conversation with Luke had left her wound up.

She decided a glass of the wine she'd uncorked for their meal might help her relax.

She took it out of the fridge, and had just poured herself a glass when Luke came into the kitchen.

'Ah-hah!' he drawled. 'Caught in the act! Well, who would have thought it—the very prim and proper Ms. McKenzie a secret drinker!'

'So,' she said flippantly, 'who're you going to tell?'

'Nobody—if you'll pour me a glass, too!'

'Finished your paperwork?'

'Yes, ma'am!'

Smiling, she poured another glass and handed it to him.

'Let's sit outside,' he said. 'I could do with a breath of fresh air.' He opened the outside door, and stood aside to let her past.

'If we sit over there, under Troy's window, we'll hear him if he cries,' she said.

Luke dragged two garden chairs across the brick patio, and set them at the far edge, in the shadows. 'How's this?'

'Lovely.' Whitney sat down. It was a beautiful evening, and the scent of nightstock sweetened the breeze. There was a new moon, and after a moment, she could see the zillion twinkling stars of the Milky Way.

'You asked if Felicia and I put off having children.'

Surprised, Whitney blinked. So...he hadn't closed the door after all. Or perhaps he had...and after thinking it over, had changed his mind. In the dusk, as she looked at him, she could see the glitter of his eyes.

She waited for him to go on.

'Our marriage was a mistake,' he said flatly. 'I soon found out we had nothing in common. I was ready to settle down—Felicia wanted to party. I wanted children—she said they'd have to wait till she was good and ready. Our marriage was empty. A farce. After four years of basically living separate lives, I told her I wanted out.'

'But...you must have made up. I mean...you have Troy.'

'Felicia begged for a second chance. She seemed so remorseful, and so committed to starting over, I agreed. She became pregnant right away. I was delighted.'

'So...what went wrong?'

'After Troy was born she was never home—and she left our son with whichever sitter was handy. She had no interest in him, spent no time with him, other than to dress him up once in a while and show him off to her friends. A party piece. I finally realized that my wife was not only unwilling to give love, but she was unable to, because there was no love in her.' His laugh was grim. 'But it wasn't till I started divorce proceedings that I found out how cold she really was.'

Far in the distance, down in the valley, Whitney could hear the hum of an engine as some large vehicle lumbered through the town of Emerald. 'She made things difficult?'

'She told me if I went through with it that she'd take me to the cleaners. She jeered that she'd only gotten pregnant because she'd known our breakup was inevitable and that if she had a baby, she'd have me over a barrel—she knew I'd pay whatever price was necessary to get sole custody.'

Luke stretched out his legs stiffly. Whitney saw the flash of a moonbeam on his glass as he raised it to gulp down his drink; and she heard the scrape of glass against brick as he set it down beside his chair.

'Which you did.'

'Which I did.'

'And Felicia...she's totally opted out of Troy's life?'

'That was the deal.'

'When did your divorce come through?'

'The day before I came home.'

Whitney brushed aside a flying insect. 'You seemed shocked, when you found out your grandmother had died—'

'I was. You see, Ramon and I had always kept in

touch, and he subscribed to the *Emerald Gazette* so I knew he'd have told me if—well, you know what they say, no news is good news.'

Silence fell between them, and Whitney sipped her wine slowly, till the glass was finally empty. Then she said, 'Why did you come back to the valley, Luke?'

'Because of Troy. I knew my grandmother wouldn't spurn my child because of our past differences. I knew she'd take us in, and I knew she'd love Troy. Just as she took you in. Just as she loved you.' His voice had become rough.

'Your grandmother died feeling no anger at you, Luke—'

'But she never tried to contact me.'

'As I explained before…she had too much pride.'

'Pride. *That damned Brannigan pride*!'

'Yes.' Whitney's voice was quiet. 'It's been responsible for a lot of Brannigan heartache.'

Neither of them spoke for a while, and the breeze, rising now, whispered restlessly through the leaves and blossoms in the garden. Whitney's heart felt wild, and strange, her emotions dangerously unstable. Moonlight, wine, and this man sitting so close—a lethal combination, affecting her in ways over which she had little control.

As always, her safety lay in retreat.

She got to her feet. 'I'm going in—'

Luke reached up and grasped her wrist. His hand was warm, his grip firm. 'Not yet.'

Her body felt on fire. Every nerve ending was aflame, every cell burned with longing. Passionately she yearned to give in…to let him pull her down onto his lap, to wind her arms around his neck, to surrender to his kiss.

And more.

Dear God, yes…more. To be his. Completely. Under the stars, in the moonlight—

She tugged her wrist free.

'We've been through this before,' she said quietly. 'Nothing has changed. Has it?' *Do you still see my mother when you look at me*? was what she was really asking.

He slumped back in his seat, and if his eyes were still open, she could no longer see the moonlight reflected in them. His face was in darkness.

He didn't answer. But he didn't need to.

Nothing had changed. Nor ever would.

Too much of the past lay between them.

Next afternoon, while Troy was napping, Whitney decided to start clearing out Cressida's desk in the library—the Chinese desk with its intricately carved grapes and vines, that she had used for her personal correspondence.

On Cressida's death, Edmund Maxwell had gone through the contents in search of business papers but had found none. He'd told Whitney that before destroying all the personal letters, she ought to read through them, just in case they contained anything of importance. It was a task she'd been putting off, but she knew it had to be done.

It felt strange, though, to sit down in Cressida's mahogany armchair, on her green velvet cushion.

Whitney couldn't count the number of times she'd come into the library and found the elderly woman seated here at her desk, her slim back as straight as a soldier's, her fine silver hair coiled in its immaculate French roll…and always, a ready smile on her lips.

Whitney's throat tightened as memories rushed in. They almost overwhelmed her, and it was with a heavy heart that she pulled down the lid, and reached for the first letter.

The next couple of hours passed quickly.

As she'd expected, Whitney found no surprises in the correspondence; and as she'd expected she found herself close to tears several times, when she read letters Cressida had received from her many friends during her illness.

She also came on a package of photographs she'd never seen before—pictures of Ben, Luke's mother Lois, and Luke. Family pictures, taken when they'd *been* a family. Would Luke want them? Or would merely looking at them be too painful for him?

She was obliged, at least, to tell him about them. If he didn't want them for himself, he should store them away for Troy. Whitney added the package to a small pile she'd mentally labeled Items To Keep.

She'd just done that when she heard sounds coming from the baby monitor on the desktop—Troy…grunting, puffing, the way he always did when he came awake after his nap. The mattress creaked as he lumbered to his feet, and she smiled as she pictured his small fingers curling around the rail, his face flushed, his expression still groggy from sleep.

Whitney closed the lid, stretched, and got to her feet.

Tonight, if Luke had no objections to her being in the library, she'd go through the remaining correspondence.

It would be a load off her mind, to have the job out of the way.

Troy was already in bed that evening, when Luke came up for dinner. As he opened the kitchen door and came in, Whitney's heartbeats gave an odd little flurry.

He'd rolled back the sleeves of his work shirt, and his shirt hung out over his jeans, which were torn at one knee and ragged at the hem. She'd never seen him look so sexy…

He tossed his ratty old straw hat on a chair, and washed his hands before sitting down at the table.

'I saw you come up from the fields,' Whitney said. 'You looked bushed.' She dished up their omelets and salad, and took her seat across from him.

'Yeah,' he said, 'it's been a hot one. So…what did you get up to this afternoon?'

'I started going through Cressida's desk,' she said. 'And I'd really like to get the job finished. Would you mind if I used the library for a while, later this evening?'

'No problem.' Luke transferred a forkful of buttery mushrooms, aswirl with cream cheese, to his mouth. For a moment, as he ate, there was silence, and then he looked up. 'Amazing. Best omelet I've ever tasted.

Don't recall my grandmother's ever dishing up this particular concoction.'

'Sean taught me how to make omelets.'

'Sean?'

'We shared an apartment, when I was at UBC. He worked weekends at The World's Greatest Omelet Factory…and he let me into some of the top chef's best-kept secrets.'

'And what did you give him in return?' Luke's eyes had a mocking gleam.

'My body.' She leveled a challenging gaze at him. 'What else?'

His laugh was spontaneous. 'Then Sean got the best of the bargain—despite the amazingness of this world-class omelet.' He sat back lazily. 'What's your price?'

'For what?'

'Passing on the secret? Same as Sean's?'

Quick fire burned Whitney's cheeks. 'I'm not sharing.'

'Let me know—' his voice had the texture of silk velvet '—if you ever decide to change your mind.'

'Don't hold your breath.'

He laughed again.

Whitney felt a warm glow suffuse her heart; she liked this feeling of rapport between them. It couldn't last forever, though; a bitter court battle still lay ahead of them.

'Find anything interesting in that desk?' Luke's tone was casual.

'It's mostly letters from friends, stuff like that, and…' She hesitated.

'And?'

'Your grandmother had a collection of…family snaps, from…when you were young. Do you want them?'

'*No.*' His answer ricocheted back faster than a speeding bullet.

In the silence that followed, she heard the steady snuffle of Troy's snoring coming from the monitor.

'When your son is older, he might want them.' She was astonished at her daring.

Luke didn't answer. Just kept doggedly eating. With his head down, so she couldn't see his expression.

She finished her omelet, and got up to make a pot of coffee. As she clicked on the switch, Luke brought over his plate and she stepped aside to give him access to the dishwasher.

When he'd swung the door up again, she expected him to move away. He didn't.

'All right,' he said impatiently. 'I'll flip through them tonight.'

'Good.' She smiled, and the moment of tension passed.

'So the monster behaved himself today?' He folded his arms and leaned back against the counter.

'He was angelic.'

'He's become very attached to you.'

'I warned you about that from the beginning. You should really have been trying, these past weeks, to find him a nanny. Somebody permanent—'

'You've grown fond of him, too.'

'That's *my* problem.' And it *was* going to be a problem; Troy had stolen her heart, and it was going to be intensely painful to say goodbye to him. She blinked away smarting tears, swiftly, so Luke wouldn't see them. Taking down two mugs, she set them on the table.

'I've been thinking…' he said slowly.

'Why is it that every time you say that,' she said with a faint smile, 'I get an ominous feeling that I'm not going to like what I'm going to hear?'

He pushed himself from the counter and moved so he was standing right in front of her. He wasn't touching her, yet awareness of him—her sexual awareness—slammed into her as if he'd hauled her against his lean, hard body.

'This is your home,' he said. 'This is where your roots are. You love the valley…but you've told me teaching jobs are very hard to come by in this area.'

'If I wanted a job teaching high school English, yes…I'd have to go where the work is. That's a cold fact of life—'

'If the will is overturned…how would you feel about staying on here?'

'Staying on? Here?'

'At Brannigan House.'

'In…what capacity?'

'You'd be lady of the house.'

Still not sure what he meant, she echoed his last words. 'Lady…of the house?'

'I'd give you room and board, and pay you to run the household—pay you very well, to look after Troy, and—'

'A *servant*? You'd ask me to cook for you, and clean for you, and wash your dirty underwear and your socks!—while you entertained Dixie Mae and all your other women—'

'Well, what the hell did you think I was offering—marriage?'

'Marriage?' Her laugh grated like slate on stone. 'I wouldn't marry you if—'

'Well, I wasn't *offering* marriage. I've had enough of marriage, thank you very much, to last me a lifetime! I wasn't even asking you to be my mistress. What I *was* offering was a home. A place to stay. Security.'

'Charity!' Whitney glared at him. 'That's what you're offering me—charity! Do you honestly think I'd stay here with you lording it over me? If the shoe were on the other foot, would you take charity from me? Don't bother to answer—I know damned well your Brannigan pride wouldn't allow you to! Well, I may not be a Brannigan, but I do have some pride. I'll never be your housekeeper...or your anything else! What I *will* be is the winner of this court case. You're going to fight? Hah! You don't even know the meaning of the word.'

It was utterly incredible that the atmosphere between them had changed so rapidly. One minute, they were almost like friends, wrapped in a warm rapport, the next, the air positively crackled with hostility. On both sides.

Luke's jaw was grimly set.

'So,' he said, glowering down at her, fine blue veins roping at his temples, 'we're back to square one, are we?'

'Darned *right* we are!'

'Then I'll see you in court.' His voice flicked over her like a whip.

CHAPTER NINE

BY THE TIME Whitney had finished her chores that evening, it was close to nine-thirty. She'd heard Luke come in from the fields half an hour earlier, so it was no surprise to hear his brusque 'Come in' when she knocked on the library door.

When she went in, he was standing at the window. He'd already showered, and changed from his work denims into a navy polo shirt and khaki shorts. He turned as she clicked the door shut behind her, and his face was shadowed.

'I've come to finish clearing out Cressida's desk,' she said coolly. 'Unless, of course, you have any objections?'

He gestured toward the desk. 'Go ahead.'

She sat down, lifted the lid…and the first thing she saw was the envelope of family pictures.

Without looking up, she held them out toward him. 'Here,' she said. 'The photos.'

After a beat, he came over, and took the package with a muttered 'Thanks.' In her peripheral vision, she was aware of his tall frame hovering close by the desk. She waited for him to move. When he didn't, she frowned and looked up.

'Troy's birthday's tomorrow,' he said gruffly.

'Oh, I didn't realize…'

He batted the heavy envelope against his thigh. 'I'm going to throw a party.'

'Well…yes. What did you have in mind?'

'A pool party—you know how he loves the water. I've asked Dix and Patsy and Beth to come up in the afternoon for a couple of hours—they all have toddlers, and it should be fun for Troy, having other kids around for a little while.'

'Yes.' And Whitney added, stiffly, 'I'll keep out of your way.'

'There's no need for you to do that,' he returned, equally stiffly. 'They'll expect you to be there.'

'Oh, I'm sure you can come up with some explanation as to why I can't attend—'

'Troy will need you…for moral support.'

Whitney drew in a sigh; how could she deny Troy the comfort of having her at his party. 'All right, I'll join in…for Troy's sake. What are you planning to serve?'

'Hot dogs, cake and ice cream. Keeping it simple is best for a one-year-old's party…according to my book.'

'Book?'

'My baby book.' A self-deprecatory grin spread over his face. 'Prescribed bedtime reading for single fathers.'

Dammit—this man got to her far too easily! Just the image of him lying in bed, brow furrowed in concentration as he pored over a chapter entitled Baby Parties, melted the anger still frosting her heart. 'Shall I bake the cake?'

'Do you want to?'

'Sure.'

'Fine,' he said. 'Thanks.'

He made to turn away, and she said impulsively, 'Luke—'

'Yeah?'

'I hate fighting.'

He raised his brows. 'It takes two to fight—'

'Yes, but it takes only one to start—'

'What's the matter? Can't take stormy weather?'

'Not,' Whitney said quietly, 'when you bring your own personal storms with you.'

She saw a dull color seep into his cheeks, but before he could reply, the doorbell rang.

'Who could that be?' She made to get up. 'I'm not expecting anyone...'

'Sit down. It'll be for me. I was telling Victoria Moss how successfully her cuttings had taken, and she said she'd drop by this evening to have a look at the vines.'

After he left, Whitney realized that the tension between them had caused her neck muscles to knot. She got up, stretched and rolled her head around to ease the aches.

Luke had dropped the envelope on the desk. She scooped it up and went over to lay it on the table by the window. As she turned to go back to the desk, a flash of movement from outside caught her eye, and when she glanced out, she saw Luke walking across the forecourt with a young woman.

So...this was Victoria Moss. Somehow, Whitney had always envisioned Ms. Moss as being much older. And plainer.

And dumpy.

Now her heart shrank, only a little, but unaccountably, as she realized how very wrong she had been.

The owner of the Sagebrush Vineyards was strikingly tall, with long black hair and a crimson silk shirt that shimmered with every thrust and jiggle of her splendid breasts. Her matching silk shorts were provocatively cut, the hem fluttering around firm, cellulite-free thighs, and accentuating the slender length of shapely tanned legs.

As she spoke to Luke, her Cleopatra features were revealed to Whitney in profile. And as she rested a hand on Luke's forearm, her body language was plain for Whitney…or anyone else…to see. Luke must be well aware that Victoria Moss was his for the taking.

Perhaps he'd already taken her.

More than once…

Stomach roiling, Whitney spun around and returned to the Chinese desk. What Luke Brannigan did—or did not—do, to—or with—Victoria Moss, was no concern of hers.

With an intensity that within minutes caused the reknotting of all her neck muscles, she threw herself into finishing her task…but soon found she couldn't concentrate. Her mind kept veering to Luke and Victoria Moss, and her heart, she acknowledged bewilderedly, was aching as it never had before. To her dismay, she felt tears spurt from her eyes, tears that dripped like raindrops onto the letter on which she'd been trying to concentrate.

Blankly, she stared at them: tears of…self-pity? But she'd never been one to indulge in that particularly dismal emotion! What was going on? What was happening to her?

Why had seeing Luke with Victoria Moss made her feel so wretched?

The answer when it came hit her like a thunderbolt from heaven—or from hell; and it had been there for her to see, for some time, only she'd never allowed herself to face it.

All these weeks, while she'd been finding herself more and more drawn to Luke, it had never occurred to her that there was more to it than mere physical attraction—more to it than desire…white-hot though that desire was.

It had gone much further than that.

Without realizing it, she had given her heart… given it completely, and forever.

To the one man in the world most unlikely to want it.

'Where did you get to last night?' Yawning, Luke poured coffee into a vacuum flask. 'Vicky wanted to meet you.'

So it was *Vicky* now. How cosy! 'I went to bed early.' Whitney spooned cereal into Troy's mouth. 'Can't believe I used to stay up till midnight on a regular basis,' she added lightly. 'A baby sure puts an end to the late nights!'

'You've adjusted well to the early-morning routine.'

'Getting up at six is for the birds!'

Luke laughed.

'What's so funny?' she demanded.

'Well, your hair does look a bit like a bird's nest! And not only are you still in your dressing gown—' he came closer and peered at her narrowly '—I do suspect you haven't even washed your face yet!'

She pushed him away. 'Your son didn't give me time,' she retorted indignantly. 'He wanted his breakfast and he wanted it now. I barely had a chance to gulp down my coffee before he started bawling.'

Coffee. It never ceased to amaze her that no matter what the existing status of their up-and-down relationship, every morning without fail Luke planted a wake-up mug of coffee on her bedside table…

Though after that first disastrous morning, he never lingered!

'Aw, come on,' he said, 'you can cope with the monster with your hands tied behind your back.'

She did find it easy caring for Troy. But wouldn't Luke be shocked if he knew how she yearned to keep him…

'Well, I'm outta here.' He screwed the lid onto the thermos and rammed the flask into his backpack. 'I'll knock off early, in time to shower before the party starts.'

He scooped up his straw hat and palmed it onto his head at a rakish angle…and as he looked down at Whitney, his cocky smile did weird things to her heart…not to mention other sensitive parts of her anatomy.

'Fine,' she said, feeling as if all the breath had been suctioned from her lungs. Swallowing hard, she turned her attention back to Troy…just in time to see him mimic his father's action by upturning his cereal bowl on his head.

Whitney put Troy down for his nap earlier than usual that afternoon, and he woke around quarter to three.

She was in his bedroom, and had just dropped him back into his crib after dressing him in a crisp yellow-and-white romper suit, when she heard a light *rat-tat* from behind.

She turned and saw Luke standing in the open doorway.

'Hi.' Sweat glistened on his forehead, and on the skin revealed by his blue open-neck shirt. 'Need any help?'

'No, everything's under control.' Except her reaction to him. She'd been feeling quite cool to this point, but now pinpricks of perspiration popped out on her upper lip.

'Where did you go to this morning?' he asked. 'I was up in the high field and I saw the car go down the road...'

'To Emerald. I needed a fancy birthday candle and some decorations for the cake...and a present for Troy.'

He leaned over the crib rail and cranked the handle of Troy's music box. 'There was a message on my answering machine,' he murmured without looking up, 'from Marilla—'

'Yes. I had a call from Edmund Maxwell. The date for the hearing has been set for—'

'July 13 next year.'

'I marked it off on my calendar.' Whitney stared

at his broad shoulders, hypnotized by the way the sweat-soaked fabric of his shirt clung to his muscles. 'It's a Friday.'

'Friday 13.' He tousled Troy's dark hair. 'Figures.'

She fought the temptation to tousle Luke's own hair in the same way. 'Will you keep an eye on Troy? I was just going to go down and set up the patio table.'

'Sure—'

She started toward the door.

'—he can come into the bathroom and watch his dad have a quick shower.'

Whitney almost stumbled as an image of Luke, naked, dazzled her mind. What a glorious sight that would be.

She didn't realise he was following her till she felt Troy's fingers grab a handful of her red hair and tug. Hard.

'Ouch!' Grimacing, she turned, to find Luke right behind her, carrying his son piggyback. She put a hand up to free herself, but Troy wasn't about to let go.

'Here,' Luke murmured, 'let me.'

He reached up to help, but even as he released her, their fingers fumbled together. The static that sparked between them made her jump. Or perhaps it wasn't static but sexual chemistry that had sent those sizzles of electricity up her arm...sizzles that intensified as with a sharply indrawn breath, Luke wove his fingers through hers and pressed her hand against his damp cheek.

Whitney's eyes jerked wide...and when she saw the swiftly darkening expression in his, she felt as if she were dropping through a trapdoor into unknown territory.

Desire—hot and fierce—pooled deep inside her. And as Luke's grip tightened, the pooling became a heavy throbbing need...a need that flared out of control when he lowered his mouth to hers.

His kiss was demanding, his taste as sweet as manna. He smelled of vines and earth, of sunshine and musk...and he was irresistible. With a moan, Whitney spread her free hand on his shirt...and became giddy as she felt the heat of his flesh, the thud of his heart, through the denim fabric.

He was in no hurry. Neither was she. She'd have been happy if the kiss had lasted through eternity and beyond.

And it might well have done, if the ringing of the doorbell hadn't suddenly jarred through the air.

At first Luke paid no heed to the bell's shrill call, only deepening his kiss as if seeking to drain the very essence of her. And not until she made a protesting sound and pushed her hand with force against his chest, did he finally release her.

He looked down at her, and though his gaze was still cloudy, it held a hint of laughter. 'To be continued at a later date,' he promised, his voice low and seductive.

Breathlessly she retorted 'Over my dead body!' and tilting her chin, stalked away—thankful he'd never know that her pulse was fluttering like leaves in a gale.

'Sorry, honey—' his teasing voice followed her

'—I'm not into necrophilia. When I kiss a woman, I prefer that woman to be very much alive—'

'Well, as long as *this* woman's alive,' Whitney called back tartly over her shoulder, 'she's going to be kicking!'

'Kicking.' His voice was rich with amusement. 'I like kicking. It's a real turn-on.'

Despite herself, Whitney smiled.

And the smile remained, along with the odd feeling that she was walking on air, as she welcomed their guests.

The party was a great success, and the happy shrieks of the children—and adults—as they splashed around in the pool might have been heard as far away as Emerald.

They ate around five, still in their swimsuits, and afterward Dixie gave the children red pails she'd brought from her day care, and within minutes had the toddlers filling the buckets with cold water from Troy's paddling pool, and making mud pies in his tree-shaded sandbox.

The others—Luke, Whitney, Patsy and Beth—relaxed on the patio, under the shade of an enormous striped umbrella.

And as Whitney sat there, a cool drink in her hand, listening while Luke chatted to the other two women, she thought how wrong she'd been in assuming that any of his old gang would ever be anything more to him now than friends. Among these former high school buddies existed the kind of ease and rapport that came from sharing a common history. From sharing memories. Happy memories.

Nothing more. But nothing less.

She shifted awkwardly in her seat as she realized Patsy and Beth had started gossiping together and Luke's attention was now focused on her.

He was sprawled lazily on his lounger, in a pair of low-slung black trunks...and as his drifting gaze lifted from her own scantily clad figure, she saw a smoldering invitation in the hazy blue depths. A bold and erotic invitation. Private but unmistakable. But even as her own eyes widened, her body clenched in involuntary response and with an urgency that shocked her. She desperately wanted to look away, but couldn't. Desperately wanted to cover herself, but didn't. Tension strummed between them like a drumroll preceding some heart-stopping event...

Luke's gaze was so penetrating she could have sworn he was able to see through the thin fabric of her bikini to the budding tips of her breasts—and beyond, to the spasms shuddering deep inside her, reaching hot dark places she had barely known existed. Swallowing hard, she tried to ignore the discomfiting but pleasurable sensations he was causing to spiral through her. To no avail. Every cell in her body was seething with a new and raw and rising excitement.

Luke cleared his throat. And from the way he suddenly dragged his towel from the arm of his lounger and draped it in rumpled folds over his lower torso, she guessed he was having his own...problems.

Problems that could only have…arisen…from an uncontrollable urge to make love to her.

Whitney's head spun. She felt as if he was making love to her already! One look from those smoldering eyes was as debilitating as the most intimate caress. An almost inaudible whimper came from her throat… and when she saw his mouth twist at the corners in a knowing smile, her face flamed. He'd heard…and interpreted…the primitive animal sound. Interpreted it as an affirmative answer to his unspoken invitation.

A shadow just outside Whitney's line of vision jerked her attention back to their surroundings. She blinked…and saw Jason, Beth's three-year-old, standing beside Luke. The child was carrying a red pail, filled almost to overflowing with water. What did he want…?

But even as Beth jumped to her feet crying 'Oh, *no*, honey—,' with a gleeful shout, Jason dumped the cold water in Luke's lap.

'Hey!' Luke growled, 'what the…?' He jerked his head around, and seeing the culprit, snaked out a hand to catch him. Too late. Giggling, Jason was already scurrying back to the sandbox, as fast as his sturdy legs could carry him.

'I think,' Patsy rose to join Beth, 'it's time to go!'

'More than!' Beth said, and laughing merrily, looped her arm through Patsy's as they made for the sandbox.

'Come on, guys,' Luke called after them good-naturedly, 'don't leave yet—it's okay, no harm done.'

But they kept going.

He slumped back in his seat, his expression wry as

he shucked the sodden towel off himself and dropped it to the deck. Whitney peeked over curiously…and somehow managed to keep her face straight. It didn't need X-ray vision to see that though the towel might have served its purpose, it was now no longer needed.

She leaned toward Luke, an expression of fake concern pasted on her face. 'Are you sure you're all right?' she whispered, her tone as hushed and grave as if he'd just made a remarkable recovery from some dread disease. 'Poor Luke…that must have been quite a…shock.'

He glowered at her…and then he threw back his head and let out a loud guffaw.

As the echo faded away, he pushed himself up from his lounger and stood over her, tall and blonde and as magnificent as a Viking warrior.

'A shock,' he said huskily, 'was exactly what was needed. But I think perhaps you could do with one, too.' His eyes had a malicious twinkle.

He tugged her from her chair, and swept her up in his arms.

And before she had time to draw breath, far less scream 'Put me down, you beast!' the beast had flung her into the deep end of the pool.

Hetty called that evening with a present for Troy.

She came to the front door, her hair upswept in its usual precarious beehive style, her plump figure bulging a little in a purple dress. Whitney invited her to come in for a cup of coffee and a slice of the birthday cake. They were in the kitchen, chatting, when Luke came in from work.

He declined Whitney's offer of coffee, saying he was going to go up and shower. He rubbed a hand against his temple as he spoke, and Hetty said,

'You got a headache, honey?'

'Yeah, a bit.'

Whitney thought he seemed paler than usual. 'Have you taken anything for it?'

He shook his head.

'Then I'll go upstairs and get you some aspirin.'

'I'm just going up,' he said. 'Where'll I find them?'

'In the medicine cabinet—in your grandmother's bathroom.' As he turned to go, Whitney gestured toward the package on the table. 'Hetty's brought something for Troy.'

'Thanks, Het.' Luke clamped a hand briefly on her shoulder. 'Nice of you to think of him.'

It was more than twenty minutes before Luke came back. He'd changed into shorts and a black T-shirt, and his hair was still damp from his shower. As he crossed to lean back against the countertop, Whitney noticed an odd tension in him that hadn't been there earlier. And she felt a pang of concern when she saw how strained his features had become.

'How's your headache?' she asked, frowning.

'Better, thanks.'

'You took aspirin?'

'A couple.' He sounded impatient. 'Headache's gone.'

Well, if it was gone, Whitney reflected uneasily, why was he looking so much paler than earlier?

'I've always liked this kitchen,' Hetty murmured, glancing around. 'I sure miss coming up here. And I miss your grandmother, Luke,' she added in a wistful tone. 'Did Whitney tell you I used to come up here once a week and do her hair? No matter how sick she felt, she wanted to look her best! A proud old lady, your gran—'

'Yeah.' Luke's nod was brusque. 'Proud she was.'

Whitney sensed he didn't want to talk about his grandmother, but oblivious to that fact, Hetty charged on.

'—but she got to confiding in me after a time—well, you know how ladies are, with their hairdressers.' She chuckled. 'It's like we're priests or something...they don't really see us as people, more like just a listening ear...'

Whitney saw Luke shift restlessly and decided to try to sidetrack the garrulous brunette. 'I always appreciated your visits, Hetty,' she said. 'It gave me a free hour to pop down to Emerald for groceries without worrying that Cressida might need me and I used to like when her church visitors came up, too.'

Hetty was not about to be sidetracked.

Her gaze was fixed steadily on Luke. 'She told me over and over how good Whitney was to her. She told me of all the long nights when Whitney would sit with her, patient and loving, hold her hand, tend to her every need—'

Embarrassed, Whitney grimaced. 'Hetty, don't—' But Hetty waved her protests away.

'Mrs. Brannigan told me,' she went on stoutly, 'that nobody in the world would ever know what an angel Whitney was. She gave up her job, a real good job, to care for her. But not only that—and this is something I heard from a friend in Penticton—when Whitney came back here to look after your gran, her fiancé threw her over—'

'Hetty, please!' Throat tightening painfully, Whitney pushed back her chair and got to her feet.

'I'm sorry, honey.' Hetty touched her arm gently. 'But Luke should know what you did for his gran, not only how you put a strain on your own health in nursing her through all those months of suffering, but your other sacrifices, too. After all, it's not every day a girl's lucky enough to get engaged to a man like Brandon McKillop—'

'Oh, damn!' Whitney crossed blindly to the sink and stared out, seeing nothing through a blur of tears.

For a long moment there was no sound in the kitchen, except for the clock on the stove and Whitney's labored breathing. Tension was as thick as a heavy fog, and she felt herself choking in it.

Luke was the one who finally broke the silence.

'Hetty,' he said quietly, 'how about you and I go for a walk, give Whitney time to clear up in here. She's had a real busy day, with the party and all. She's tired out.'

'Sure.' Hetty's voice quavered. 'Sure, Luke.' She hesitated, and then said, 'Bye then, Whitney.'

Whitney could hardly speak, her throat felt so constricted, but she managed a husky, 'Bye, Hetty.'

After they'd left, she stumbled to the nearest chair and sat down, her emotions tearing her heart till she felt as if it were in shreds. She'd had little time to think about her broken engagement when Cressida was alive...and after her death, with Luke's moving in and a baby to look after, the immediate past had been shoved into a far corner of her mind.

Now she drew it forward and looked at it squarely.

Brandon McKillop had been a mistake. If he'd loved her, he would have supported her in her decision to look after Cressida, instead of issuing his harsh ultimatum:

It's her or me, babe. I want to get married, and I want to get married now. I'm not about to wait around while you play nursemaid to somebody who could live for another ten years.

She'd tried to tell him how much she owed Cressida, but he'd refused to listen. Till then, she'd been convinced she loved him, but when he'd revealed his selfishness and lack of compassion, she realized she'd never really known him.

She hadn't felt one twinge of regret over their breakup.

Why, then, was she now feeling so upset and miserable? Was it because, by her uncontrolled emotional reaction to Hetty's words, she had surely conveyed to Luke the erroneous impression that she was still in love with her ex-fiancé?

But what of it! Luke's own feelings for her were carnal—nothing else. Besides, even if he'd been tempted to feel more, a wall of glass stood between them, so when he looked at her, all he saw was the reflection of her mother.

Oh, how she wished—desperately wished—that it was in her power to shatter that glass!

* * *

Half an hour later, Whitney heard Hetty's pink Caddy chug away down the driveway.

She'd just finished setting the table for the next day's breakfast when Luke returned to the kitchen. She braced herself, not wanting to talk. To her surprise he just stood in the doorway and stared at her, in a peculiarly dark and brooding way that made the hair at her nape stand on end.

'Luke? What…is it?'

'Was that true, what Hetty said? You were engaged?'

'Yes, I was engaged—for several months.'

'To McKillop ComputerSuperStores?'

'No,' she said with exaggerated patience, 'to Brandon McKillop *of* McKillop ComputerSuperStores.'

'Where did you meet him?'

'Through a friend of mine who teaches at Penticton High.'

'You never mentioned a broken engagement!' He threw the accusatory words at her as if they were small hard stones.

She zinged back at him with perfect aim: 'Because it was none of your damned business!'

'You should have told me! And you should have told me *exactly* what the situation was here. Why in God's name didn't you hire a live-in nurse to care for my grandmother?'

'She didn't want a nurse!'

'Figures,' he muttered, and then glared at her again. 'The man's worth millions!'

He was back to talking about Brandon McKillop.

'It's only money, Luke,' she said wearily. She could have told him it wasn't Brandon's money, but his tremendous drive and his dark good looks and his single-minded pursuit of her that had eventually won her over.

'Only money...' He shook his head helplessly, as if only now did he finally realize that she wasn't the gold digger he'd always believed her to be.

'I'm not saying money isn't important, Luke. But there are other things that are much more important.'

'Yeah.' He sounded tired. Reaching into his shirt pocket, he took out a clear plastic container with some pink pills jumbled in the bottom. 'I found this in the medicine cabinet when I was looking for the aspirin.' He held it out.

Whitney frowned. 'What is it?'

'The bottle of sleeping pills Dr. McKay prescribed for my grandmother, two days before she had her accident.'

Whitney took the container, and shook it to sort out the pills; they rattled like hailstones on a tin roof.

'You don't need to count them,' Luke said grimly. 'There are twelve. McKay prescribed fourteen...'

'Ah.' Whitney heaved a huge sigh of relief. 'So I couldn't have given Cressida any when she came home from hospital! Well, I *am* glad about that!'

'You don't see the significance of this, do you?'

'Significance?'

'These twelve pills, along with Hetty's unbiased account of your devotion to my grandmother—up to and including the sacrifice you made when you put her well-being before your opportunity to marry a millionaire—have blown my case right out of the water.'

'What are you saying, Luke?'

'What I'm saying is this. I plan on withdrawing my Statement of Claim first thing tomorrow. The estate is yours, just as my grandmother wanted it to be.

'And I'll be moving out just as soon as I find a job.'

CHAPTER TEN

WHITNEY spent a sleepless night, and next day, saw little of Luke.

That evening, hot, restless and out of sorts, she decided to go upstairs and have a shower to cool off.

She'd just come out of the bathroom, in her robe and undies, when she heard a brisk knock on her bedroom door.

Frowning, she padded across to open it.

Luke was standing there, hands in the back pockets of his jeans, fine gold hair gleaming at the open neck of his shirt...and his lean features were drawn.

'Thought I'd just tell you,' he said, 'Vicky's been looking for an assistant manager for the Sagebrush Vineyards and she let me know tonight that the job's mine if I want it. I may take her up on her offer. Pay's not great, but beggars can't be choosers.'

Whitney felt a ripple of panic. 'You know you can stay on here—'

'Charity, Whit?' Luke's expression was self-derisive. 'I think we've hit this topic before...'

'It wouldn't be charity. It could be a...partnership.'

'Charity.'

'You'd rather work for Victoria Moss than—'

'For you? Damned right!'

'But you could still *live* here.'

'A cabin goes with the job.'

'What about Troy? You'll have to put him in day care!'

A nerve flickered in his cheek. 'I'll hire a nanny.'

'But he's used to *me*!' she said urgently. 'I'll look after him for you, Luke. Sagebrush is only a half-hour drive from here. You could drop him off in the morning, and I could drive him back in the evening.'

'For God's sake, Whitney, you know the hours I work! I start at five-thirty in the morning, and I'm rarely finished before nine at night! I appreciate your offer, but if I get the job, I'm going to need somebody to live in.'

'You can't take him, Luke, he's so happy here.' Whitney felt her eyes burn, felt tears threaten. Sniffing in an attempt to keep them at bay, she rubbed her nose…but as she did, a large tear splashed onto the back of her hand. 'Please, don't do this.' Her voice was raspy with emotion.

'Look, I know how you feel, but— Oh, hell, Whitney, don't cry.'

But it was too late. Choking on a sob, Whitney stumbled back across the room and sank onto the edge of the bed, her face buried in her hands. She couldn't bear to lose Troy. But she couldn't bear to see Luke go, either—especially couldn't bear to see him move to Sagebrush where Victoria Moss would—

Her shoulders shook, and her sobs came thick and fast. Her throat felt as if a rough rope was slowly and painfully tightened around it.

The mattress dipped as Luke sat down beside her.

'Don't cry, Whit,' he pleaded. He pulled her against

his chest and wrapped his strong arms around her. 'Please don't cry.'

Somehow, after a few false starts, she finally managed to control her sobbing.

Luke tilted her chin up, and with the pads of his thumbs, wiped the damp of the tears from her flushed cheeks.

'Better?' he murmured.

She nodded, unable to drag her gaze from his, and as their eyes locked, the sexual tension that always pulsated between them, just below the surface, suddenly exploded out of the blue with a power that rocked her.

And obviously rocked Luke, too. His gaze widened, and for a stark moment he stared at her as if stunned. And then, drawing in a sharp breath, his eyes aglitter with desire, he grasped her shoulders tightly and claimed her lips with his own.

She closed her eyes, blocking out everything but the taste of him, the scent of him, the nearness of him, and felt every cell in her body leap in eager joyful response to his hungry kiss.

She didn't resist as he guided her backward, nor did she resist when he continued to kiss her, his caresses becoming more and more passionate, more and more seductive. But when he slid her robe down over her upper arms, a shudder trembled through her. And he was as deeply affected as she. She heard the sudden change in his breathing, heard it become ragged as he skimmed his fingertips over her breast—heard it quicken as he felt the peak rise under his searching touch.

By the time he started undoing the front catch of her bra, she felt as intoxicated as if she'd been drinking champagne…and just as uninhibited. The catch gave easily. Her breasts rose free from their lacy confinement, and she heard Luke's whispered adoration.

As his lips found their goal, wave after wave of sensation rippled through her, to a place quivering deep and low inside her. She moaned, and the sound drew an answering groan from Luke.

Even with her eyes closed, she knew he was taking off his jeans, his shirt. Then he eased off her robe, and somehow removed her bra without getting all tangled in the narrow satin straps.

He pulled her close, and she felt the rasp of his hair-roughened skin against her naked breasts. Coils of tension spiraled low, causing tiny muscles to clench, sensitized flesh to become swollen and inflamed. Involuntarily, wantonly, she pressed herself to him.

And that was when she realized, with a gulp, that nothing was between them now but her bikini panties. A scrap of yellow cotton, with a white pattern of daisies…

'Look at me, Whitney.' His voice was strained.

She took in a shaky breath, and slowly opened her eyes.

'Are you sure?' His blue gaze was cloudy, unfocused.

She nodded—couldn't have spoken for the lump in her throat—but a tremor quivered through her heart. He knew she'd been engaged; he would assume she was an experienced lover. How was he going to react when he discovered—

He lowered his face to her breast, and his lips, with exquisite tenderness, again caressed the aching tips. Bliss. Ecstasy. Her mind seemed to have ceased functioning. Oh, she knew that while he teased her with soft kisses, he was also taking off her panties, but she cared nothing for that. All she cared about was that he mustn't stop, mustn't stop this exquisite torture, or she would die.

He seemed to have no intention of stopping. He paid homage to her breasts till she was threshing her head from side to side, begging him for she knew not what—some kind of release—begging him to please, please…

Then just when she thought she had reached pleasure's peak, he slid his hand down over her belly, slid it low, to where dark red hair curled silkily over her dainty feminine mound.

She drew in a panicky breath…but as she did, she caught his wild-animal scent, and need overcame her panic, to rush through her in a dizzying torrent. Achingly she yearned for him to trespass further, but as if aware of her impatience and determined to continue his exquisite torture, he let his hand linger, subtly moving, subtly circling—inexorably spinning her into an even more advanced state of delirium, till she couldn't contain a desperate whimper, couldn't control the desperate shudder raking through her.

Signs of total surrender. Luke must surely have been waiting for them, for his body became taut, and with a low growl, he at last—at last!—slid his hand down.

And touched where no man had ever touched before.

Whitney froze. Though longed for, this intimate caress…this trespass on the most tender part of her…was a devastating shock to her innocence. But even as she parted her lips in a silent gasp, Luke teased the quivering bud with his fingertips, stimulating it with featherlight flutterings; and tormenting her with daring little forays as if searching out the secrets of a soft-petaled rose. A rose moist now with dew, and opening to the sun. Faint with rapture, giddy with wonder, Whitney threw her head back. What kind of magic was this? Her pulses pounded, her nerves drummed, and nothing existed for her but sensation.

'Are you ready?' he whispered, his breath warm on her neck. She heard a sound of arousal come from deep in her throat. He was so clever, so very clever. Those fingers, so…oh…

'Yes—' her response was urgent, breathless '—oh, yes, yes, Luke, I'm ready…'

He kissed her on the mouth, a hard, possessive kiss, and then he covered her. She felt the jut of his arousal as he guided himself between her thighs, and she tensed; felt her heart stop as he encountered the barrier between them—

His shock was profound. Every muscle in his body clenched dramatically; his hissed-in oath revealed his dismay. For one terrible moment, she thought he was going to draw back…but before he could, she arched up against him with an imperative cry...and with a hoarse and helpless groan he drove into her.

The pain of his entry was sharp, but her protest of distress was drowned out by his delving kiss...and soon all thought of discomfort was forgotten as pleasure took over.

Nothing in her experience had prepared her for the dazzling journey on which he guided her, a journey that took her to the brink of ecstasy, many times over, before he gave in to her anguished pleas for release. He flew her up to one last soaring height, and then swept her over the edge, to fall into space and drift in trembling slow-motion back to a land that would never again be the same.

And even as she lay there, light-headed and limp, Luke, too, reached that vertiginous pinnacle, before slumping down on top of her with a prolonged groan of pleasure-drenched fulfillment.

'I love you,' he murmured. 'Oh, Whitney, my darling angel...I love you...'

He shifted his weight from her body, and lay on his side, facing her. He pulled her to him. He held her tight, her cheek against his heart, and she could hear the rapid *thud-thud* of his heartbeat, a counterpoint to her own.

'Are you all right?' he whispered.

'Oh, yes,' she said against his chest. 'More than.'

He nodded, sleepily. 'Good,' he said, and momentarily tightened his hold, before slackening it again.

Within minutes, his breathing had steadied, and had become deeper. She knew he was asleep.

He loved her. The glory of it made her heart sing.

She wanted to get up, throw open the window and shout the news down the valley, till the people heard her as far away as Emerald.

But she didn't want to waken Luke.

So instead she lay quietly in his arms, drawing in the mingled scents of sex and naked flesh and sweat-damp sheets.

And thinking she'd never been happier in her life.

She woke next morning to the sound of rushing water.

And with a blush, pictured Luke in the shower, rinsing off the signs and the scents of their love-making. The memories—her lips curved in a dreamy smile—would linger…

Murmuring a contented sigh, she stretched, and as she did, became aware that her body was aching in places it had never ached before. She sat up; felt hot and sticky; gave an impatient wriggle…

Perhaps she should join Luke in the shower.

Pulses fluttering, she got up and padded across the carpet to the bathroom. The door was ajar, and stealthily she pushed, holding her breath. The shower curtain was of transparent vinyl with pencil-thin stripes of navy and red. Through it she could see Luke, his tall lean frame gauzed by steam as he stood under the hot spray. His back was to the showerhead, his hands running through his blond hair as he rinsed away the last vestiges of shampoo.

The sound of the spray drowned out any noise Whitney might have made as she slipped past the edge of the shower curtain; and Luke could have had no idea she was there, right behind him, till she leaned her breasts against his back and slid her arms around his waist.

He stiffened. And remained stiff as she glided her hands up his ribs and splayed her fingers over his chest. Under her fingertips, she felt soft peaks become taut.

'Good morning,' she whispered through the water streaming down her face from above. She teased the small brown nubs, running her fingertips over them, back and forth, the same way he'd driven her crazy the night before.

Her breath caught as he threw his head back. She thought she heard a dark sound, an animal sound, come from his throat, and it roused her unbearably.

She skimmed her fine-boned hands down his ribs, down over his belly, and—

He grasped her wrists, his hands trembling a little, and stopped her. 'No.' His words had a strangled quality.

Whitney's chuckle was throaty. 'So you can dish it out but can't take it, huh?' She pressed kisses against his back, her lips lingering on his warm wet flesh.

'Whitney, stop.' There was an edge of desperation to his voice. 'Please.' He shrugged off her caresses, and at the same time released her wrists, letting her hands drop. He swept back the shower curtain and stepped out of the stall. Her gasp of distress was drowned out by the sound of the rushing water.

'*Luke*?'

He turned, slowly, and met her anguished gaze. 'Last night,' he said, his voice so low as to be almost inaudible, 'should never have happened. I'm sorry, Whitney.'

Stark-eyed, she watched as he took a towel from the rail and went out, pulling the door shut behind him.

She stayed there, under the shower, till the water ran cold, her mind in a turmoil of bewilderment, her heart lanced with pain. How could Luke have changed so, within the space of a few hours?

When she returned to the bedroom, he'd gone. The window had been flung wide open and the mattress lay bare. He had stripped the slips from the pillows and the stained sheets from the bed. His clothes were gone; the white towel nowhere to be seen. Her robe and undies were missing. All reminders of last night wiped out as if it had never been.

But...he had told her he loved her.

Was that something men felt they had to say, after despoiling a virgin? Did that, in their eyes, make it all right?

But Luke had never lied to her before. Why would he lie to her about that? She cast her eyes despairingly around the room as if seeking an answer to her question...

And saw the picture.

The picture of her mother, Krystal, and Ben.

For the past weeks, the framed snapshot had been lying on the dresser where she'd set it. If Luke had ever noticed it, he'd never mentioned it...but his morning visits to her room to deliver her coffee were always on the run; she doubted he'd ever taken time to glance around.

This morning, however, when he'd awakened, he must have taken the time to look around. And he had seen the picture.

Oh, it was still on the dresser.

Facedown.

A bitter tear escaped and trickled down her cheek.

So now she knew why Luke had rejected her. In the dark, he'd been able to ignore the past. He'd been able to walk through that wall of glass as if it didn't exist. But this morning, in the light of day, he couldn't even bear to look at her…

Because if he did, he would see her mother.

He had gone to the fields by the time she brought Troy downstairs, but when she checked the laundry room, she found he'd been busy. All the items he'd taken from her bedroom were now in the washing machine—towel, clothes and bed linen; whites, darks and coloreds—haphazardly tossed in together as if he couldn't wait to be rid of them.

In the afternoon, she took Troy to a children's park on the outskirts of Emerald, down by the lake. Later, she shopped for groceries. They arrived home around five…and on the kitchen table, she found a scrawled note: Having dinner with Victoria Moss. Luke.

As mindlessly as a robot, she fed Troy and herself, played with the child for a while and then put him to bed. The evening was hot, and she found she could settle to nothing. When bedtime rolled around, she knew she wouldn't sleep and decided to go for a swim in the moonlight, in the hope of tiring herself out. Slipping into a bikini, she took the baby monitor out to the patio, placed it on the patio table and dived into the pool.

She had swum thirty laps, and was climbing exhausted up the steps at the deep end, when she heard a sound above.

Already breathless, when she glanced up and saw Luke standing at the poolside she found it almost impossible to get the necessary air into her lungs. She had not expected to see him…had half-expected him to stay away all night.

He was wearing a white dress shirt, fancy tie and a pair of navy dress pants. His cuffs were rolled back, the knot in his tie slackened, the top button of his shirt undone. Dressed, she decided, to kill.

Was there lipstick on his collar? she wondered acidly.

He handed her the peach-and-gold beach towel she'd left on the pool apron, and stepped back.

She blotted her wet hair with the towel, and started patting her shoulders dry.

'Would you like a drink?' he asked.

Why not! Drown the old sorrows, right? 'Sure.'

'White wine?'

'Whatever you're having,' she said carelessly.

He came back with two glasses of wine.

Whitney tossed down her towel and sank onto the nearest lounger. She accepted her glass of wine, and thanked heaven that the smell of chlorine from her hair was strong enough to overpower any scent that might be wafting from Luke's hair or clothes—whether that perfume might be expensive, and packaged in France; or musky and unique to Luke himself.

With a haughty lift of one shoulder, she turned and set the glass on the table at her side.

That was when, in the moonlight, she noticed the roses. White roses, in a crystal vase. It looked as if there might be a dozen.

'For me?' she asked, raising her brows...but concealing her very real surprise.

He nodded, and sat down opposite her, in an upright strapped chair.

'Men usually bring flowers when they want to apologize,' she said coolly. 'So...what's the occasion, Luke?'

Dull color rose to his cheeks. 'Don't make this more difficult than it already is, Whitney—'

'Red roses for love...white for despoiling a virgin.' Her laugh was bitter. 'A dozen white roses. Cheap at the price, Luke.'

'Whitney, I—'

Whitney shot to her feet and snatched the roses from the vase, immune to the pain as the thorns ripped her skin. 'You should have saved your money!' she cried, running to the pool and hurling the long-stemmed flowers out into the water. 'I don't want your damned roses!'

Breasts heaving, she stood with her back to him, every line of her body screaming her outrage and anger.

She heard his sigh, and it was a weary sound. She also heard the scrape of his chair as he got to his feet.

'I've taken the job at Sagebrush,' he said. 'Vicky and I'll be getting together to sign a contract at the end of the week. The cabin is small, but—'

'It's my mother, isn't it.' Anger spent, outrage dissipated, Whitney turned and looked at him, her voice as weary as his sigh had been. 'Still my mother, between us.'

'You're wrong—'

'I'm not! You turned the picture facedown—the picture in my room—I saw it!'

He shook his head. 'I did look at the picture, and it fell over as I set it down. I just didn't bother to set it up again.' His twisted smile was ironic. 'I only saw your mother once, and my memories of her were…the memories of a distraught teenager. The likeness is only superficial—I know that now. Oh, the coloring may be the same and the features, but there's a world of difference in the eyes; yours are clear, and filled with integrity, while hers—'

'Then what?' Whitney pleaded, brushing aside his words. 'If not that, then what?' She inhaled a shivering breath. 'Last night, Luke, you said…you loved me.'

'Last night was a mistake—*my* mistake, and one I deeply, deeply regret. For God's sake, Whitney.' Anguish tore his voice. 'You know my financial situation—do you honestly believe that under the present circumstances I could ever ask you to become my wife? I have my pride!'

Whitney stared at him incredulously…and then rocked back as if he'd slapped her. 'You mean—'

'That's it, darlin'.' His words were grim, and threaded with self-mockery. 'It's that ol' Brannigan pride again. And there's nothin' you, or anybody else, can do about it.'

Whitney felt utterly defeated. Utterly, utterly defeated. Any attempt to change Luke's mind would, she knew, be a lost cause. The pain she felt in her heart was so intense she almost hunched over. Instead she straightened her spine, and fixed him with a steady gaze.

'You're right,' she said, keeping her sorrow hidden. 'There's nothing I can do about it…and I won't even try. I learned a long time ago that a Brannigan lets nothing stand in the way of his pride.'

But during the sleepless hours of that night, she came up with a solution to the problem, a solution so perfect in its simplicity she wondered why it had never occurred to her before.

She was awake, and waiting, next morning when Luke dropped off her coffee.

As he turned and made for the door, she called after him, 'Hang on a sec.'

Dragging the sheet up to her chin, she pushed herself up on one elbow. He paused, and turned.

'I have to go out later today,' she said. 'Can you come up early, and look after Troy till I get back?'

'Sure, no problem.' His tone was flat. 'What time?'

'Four-thirty.'

'Okay.' He hesitated, and then, frowning, said, 'Can I ask where you're going?'

'I've something I want to do, in Emerald.' She had tried to sound casual; instead she sounded evasive, and felt a rush of guilty color flood her cheeks.

His lips tightened. 'Don't do anything foolish.'

'I don't intend to—'

'Are you going to see Edmund Maxwell?' he barked.

'What if I am?' How on *earth* had he guessed?

Fury burned in his eyes. 'You're wasting your time! My grandmother left the estate to you and no piece of paper you manufacture is going to make a difference to the way I feel.' He clenched his hands into tight fists. 'Don't even *think* of insulting me by signing over the estate to me—my God, I can see by your stunned expression that that's exactly what you were planning to do!'

Whitney buried her face in her pillow. She'd planned to present him with a fait accompli. Now her plans were in smithereens. But she should have known better. She knew what kind of a man he was.

'I still plan on going out,' she said, her voice half muffled by the pillow, 'so you'll have to look after Troy.'

'Fine.'

She listened, her breathing erratic, as he stomped away along the corridor, and ran heavily down the stairs.

The whole house reverberated as he slammed the front door behind him.

Luke came up at four-thirty as arranged, and with barely a word passing between them, she handed Troy over and left.

She drove into Penticton, had dinner, saw a movie and set off for the drive back to the valley. It was close to eleven by the time she got home.

She got out of the car and walked around toward

the back, intending to let herself in by the kitchen door, but just as she reached the corner, she heard someone talking on the patio. Luke. But who was with him?

She hesitated. If Victoria Moss was his visitor, a quick retreat was in order; the last person she wanted to see was that woman! But after a moment, she realized Luke's voice was the only one—he must be talking on the cordless phone.

'Thanks again, Vicky, for your offer of a job, but as I said, I wanted to call and let you know I won't be needing it now after all. The Emerald Valley Vineyards are mine...'

What? About to move forward, Whitney stood stock-still. And listened. Incredulously. Shamelessly.

'...or as good as,' Luke went on. 'I can hardly believe she came through after all, though for a while there, I really thought—' he chuckled wryly, as if at some comment coming across the line. 'Yeah, Vicky—a way with women. You either have it or you don't! At any rate, once Whitney and I have our little talk, I guess we'll have to take a trip to the lawyer's office to sign a few papers and then the vineyards will legally be mine. At last.'

Whitney put a trembling hand against the wall of the house to steady herself, and then blindly felt her way back to the front door, hardly able to see for her scalding tears. What a wonderful actor Luke was! His show that morning, when he'd told her he'd turn down the estate if she tried to turn it over to him, had truly convinced her.

A way with women indeed! Oh, she had to admit

he could charm an eagle from its aerie...but this was one bird no longer under his spell!

Without a sound she let herself in the front door and crept up the stairs. She got ready for bed in the dark, and a few minutes later was lying curled up under the covers.

She thought she heard Luke come upstairs half an hour later; thought she heard him call her name, knock lightly on her door.

But she lay still, breathing softly and evenly, and after a time, the house was silent again.

To her bewilderment, Luke kept to his usual routine the next morning. He dropped off her coffee and didn't linger, and by the time she went downstairs, he'd left for the fields.

He didn't come in for lunch, but then he rarely did. Still, if he expected to be making that trip to the lawyer, why hadn't he made himself available so she could give him the news he expected—the 'news' that she had, despite his protestations, signed the estate over to him? Was it part of his plan to play the wide-eyed innocent when she broke it to him? Boy, did he ever have a shock in store!

It was around five when she heard his truck rumbling up the driveway. She was in the backyard with Troy, and as she heard the engine cut off, she held her breath, wondering if Luke might seek her out.

He didn't.

At least, not then, but he did half an hour later.

She was weeding a small rose bed, while Troy played a few feet away in his sandbox. Her heart went *boomtity-boom* as she heard the patio door slide open and then shut again.

Showdown time.

'Hi, there.' Luke's voice preceded him as he crossed the lawn toward them.

She sat back on her heels, and watched him approach. He'd showered and changed from his work clothes into a pair of khaki chinos and a wheat-colored sports shirt. Her own slacks were grubby, her shirt damp under the arms and across her back. Not that it mattered. This was not a man she needed to impress.

'Finished for the day?' she asked, her tone cool.

'Yup, taking the evening off.' His words were casually spoken, but she thought they had an edge of suppressed excitement...and in his eyes was a glint she'd never seen there before. A glint she couldn't read. Somehow—even though she knew she had the upper hand—it made her feel uneasy...

With a happy 'Dada!' Troy clambered out of the sandbox, and Luke swung him up on his wide shoulders. Troy latched onto his father's thatch of fair hair, and as a chuckling Luke scooped a big hand under Troy's padded bottom to support him, a lump rose in Whitney's throat. She tried to swallow it, but the uncomfortable feeling persisted.

'What time's dinner?' Luke asked.

'It's just chicken salad,' she said. 'We can have it anytime.'

'Let's go in then.'

'Sure.' She dropped her trowel, and pushed herself to her feet.

'You were late home last night,' Luke said, as they walked across the lawn. 'I didn't hear you come in.'

'Did you wait up?' she asked artlessly.

'Matter of fact, I did.' They had reached the patio; he pulled the sliding door open for her.

'I was home by eleven, but the house was in darkness, so I crept upstairs quietly so as not to waken anybody.' As she walked by him, the scent of his spicy aftershave stirred disturbingly erotic memories. Ruthlessly she quashed them.

'I waited out here on the patio.' He stepped in behind her and slid the door shut.

'Ah.' She made her way through to the kitchen. 'Did you want to see me about something?'

'I did, actually—'

She stopped short just inside the kitchen door and swung around so fast he almost bumped into her. 'Something important?'

'Yes.' The glint had gone from his eyes, and in the blue depths there was such an intensity she almost shivered.

'Concerning…what?'

'Us.'

'Us?'

Troy banged his father's ears with his clenched fists. 'Ouch!' Luke growled. 'Hey…let's get you down from there. We need some serious disciplining here… Excuse me, Whitney, I'm going to lock him up in his chair!'

Whitney stepped aside, leaning weakly against the counter as Luke strapped Troy into the high chair. She was no good at these games…and had no patience for them! She wanted to scream at him to get to the point, so she could tell him, triumphantly, that she knew everything and there was no way she'd ever sign the estate over to him.

But Troy's interruption seemed to have distracted his train of thought.

They sat down to dinner, and during the meal, the conversation was general. Luke did mention that the first tiny grapes had appeared, and that the crop looked as though it would exceed even their most optimistic estimations.

'Reason for rejoicing,' Whitney remarked, her gaze level as she looked at him. His answering smile was bland.

As soon as they finished eating, he whisked Troy out of his chair, and said he'd put him to bed.

'Let's have our coffee in the library for a change,' he said as he went out of the room. 'I won't be long.'

As she wiped off the counter, Whitney caught a glimpse of her reflection in the chrome kettle, and a frustrated sigh escaped her. Her hair had been flattened by the sun hat she'd been wearing outside; her blouse was creased; her nose shiny. She could nip up to her bedroom and freshen up.

She tightened her lips. Her purpose was not to seduce, she reminded herself grimly.

Her purpose was to annihilate.

CHAPTER ELEVEN

'THE CABIN that goes with the assistant manager's job at the Sagebrush Vineyards—is it furnished?'

Whitney's question came out calmly, but it had not been formulated calmly in her mind. She and Luke had almost finished their coffee, and so far, he had made no move to bring up the subject of the will. And as she'd watched him lounging in his leather armchair by the window, as if he had all the time in the world, she'd felt a surge of temper—temper that had swiftly escalated till she'd been forced to ask the leading question or burst.

'Funny you should mention it.' He set his coffee mug on the windowsill. 'It is furnished, but sparsely...and when Vicky showed me the living room, I saw immediately that something was missing.' He nodded toward Cressida's desk. 'One of those.'

'But surely you'll have the use of an office?'

'Oh, yeah, there's a modern office in the winery building...but I thought I'd like a desk at home for my personal use.' An odd light glinted in his eyes, similar to the glint that had made Whitney uneasy earlier. Was that *laughter* she was seeing there? *Smug* laughter? Did Luke find it amusing to toy with her this way? She felt a hard knot of anger form in her chest...

'Well,' he went on lazily, 'what I decided was I'd ask you to let me have my grandmother's desk. You wouldn't miss it, would you, since you've never used it?'

Oh, he was a game-player—still pretending that he expected to be moving to the Sagebrush Vineyards. But she'd go along with him...for the moment. 'Sure,' she said easily, guilelessly, 'you can have it. Anything else?'

'No, I just wanted the desk—'

Ah-ha! A slip, though a minor one. Had he still expected to leave, he'd surely have said, 'I just *want* the desk.'

'—because it has special meaning for me.' Getting to his feet, he walked over to the desk and ran an affectionate hand over the dark wood with its ornamental carvings. 'My grandmother and I used to leave messages for each other in the secret drawer.'

'Secret drawer?'

He quirked a brow. 'She never told you about it, when *you* were a child? You didn't leave notes for each other?'

'No, I know nothing about any secret drawer.'

'Well, I'll be—' Luke drew a hand over his eyes, but not before Whitney had caught a glimpse of his expression and saw that he was deeply moved. 'I'd have thought she'd have let you in on it, too.' His voice was gruff. 'It was a game she enjoyed...we both enjoyed. I'd leave my report card there for her to find, she'd hide my birthday money...'

Whitney allowed herself to feel a momentary compassion for him. 'She must have cherished that closeness between you. You were very special to her, Luke…and were, till the day she died. Despite your estrangement, her love for you never wavered. But I think you already know that.'

'If I hadn't known it already, I—' He drew in an abbreviated breath and planted a hand on top of the desk. 'I'm getting ahead of myself. Whitney, I said earlier that I wanted to talk to you about…us.'

Whitney put down her mug on the side table, and clasped her hands together in her lap. Here it came, the moment she'd been waiting for. Her heartbeat picked up speed, and she braced herself.

'Two nights ago,' he said huskily, 'we made love…'

It was the last thing she'd expected him to say. And she was totally thrown off balance by his referring to what had happened between them as making love. Not having sex.

'…and the next morning, I rejected you—'

'Because I own the vineyards.' The words came out stiffly.

'Because of my pride.'

'Go on.'

'Whitney, if the vineyards had been mine, instead of rejecting you, I would have asked you to be my wife.'

And now he expected her to say, 'Darling, the vineyards are yours! I signed them over to you this afternoon!'

Nausea swam through her; she had no stomach for this.

Wearily she rose to her feet.

'Don't go on, Luke. I know you'll be shocked... and disappointed...to hear this, but I didn't, after all, relinquish my ownership of the estate. Actually—' her laugh was dry, and mirthless '—you only have yourself to blame. Your act, this morning, was so convincing, I truly believed you meant it, when you said you wanted no part of the place, at least not that way...'

He was staring at her, a blank look on his face. She could see she had truly shocked him.

'I heard you talking to Victoria Moss on the phone last night,' she went on, 'I heard you tell her the estate was as good as yours, and that I'd come through after all. Did you tell her, Luke, that you had to sleep with me to get what you wanted?'

Where was the expected surge of triumph? All she felt was a numbness, in her heart and in her soul.

But he...oh, Luke wouldn't feel numb! Thwarted in his plans, he would lash out at her mercilessly, in that cruel way she'd come to know so well.

Tears pricked her eyes, and she turned; she was going to cry, and he mustn't know. But she'd taken only two steps toward the door, when she heard him come after her. Her heart gave a panicky leap, and she broke into a run.

He caught up with her in the hallway, just as she reached the foot of the stairs; he grasped her shoulder and pulled her around.

Fearfully, cringing, she looked up at him, but when she saw the look in his eyes, her mind staggered in bewilderment. She could see no anger there, only tenderness. Tenderness so sweet, so beguilingly sweet, she felt she surely must be dreaming.

'You idiot,' he murmured, 'you darling, beautiful idiot.' He cupped her face in his hands. 'How could I have fallen for such a foolish creature?'

'It won't work,' she whispered brokenly, 'not with all the sweet talk in the world. I won't give you the vineyards, Luke. It's not what your grandmother wanted. So your little scheme was in vain. You could have saved yourself the hardship of sleeping with me—'

'Oh, yeah.' Amusement glistened in his eyes. 'Some hardship.' He kissed her lips, lips that were moist with tears. 'Whitney, listen to me…'

No, she wouldn't listen. She wouldn't allow him to woo her with his winning ways. She might want him, but she could never love him, knowing he had such a devious streak. But he was so very difficult to resist…

'My darling.' His eyes continued to adore her. 'Last night, when you were out, I found another will. A later will.'

So busy was she, trying to keep her body unyielding, that for a moment what he said didn't sink in. Even when it did, it didn't make sense.

'A…nother will? A…later will?' She sounded like a mentally challenged parrot.

'Yes.' He grinned. 'A…nother will. A…later will. This one handwritten, dated a month after the first, and witnessed by two of my grandmother's church visitors, whereas the original one was typed, and witnessed by Edmund and Charles Maxwell.'

Her eyes were wide. 'But...where was it? Edmund Maxwell went through every drawer—'

'Every drawer,' Luke said softly, 'except the one only Cressida and I knew about.'

Whitney drew in a gasp. 'The secret drawer!'

'Come.' He took her hand, and led her back into the room, across to the desk. And he guided the tip of her index finger to the smallest grape, in an elegantly carved bunch of grapes, on the side of the desk.

'There,' he said. 'Press.'

Whitney pressed, and her mind boggled as a long narrow drawer swung forward.

In it, she saw an envelope. It was addressed to Luke.

'That's it?' she asked, her voice shaking a little. 'The...second will?'

He picked up the envelope, slipped out a single sheet of paper and handed it to her.

In an increasingly dazed state, Whitney read every closely written word...and saw that though the minor bequests remained unchanged, Cressida had left the Emerald Valley Vineyards to Luke.

And to her 'beloved Whitney McKenzie: Brannigan House and the contents therein.'

Whitney's head spun and she felt a light floating joy. Oh, not because the house now belonged to her, though she had always loved it dearly. What she cared about was that Luke hadn't deceived her after all.

'So when you were talking to Victoria about having a way with women,' she said, 'you were referring—teasingly—to the relationship you had with your grandmother.'

'And when I talked about someone "coming through," I was referring to her having left me the vineyards.'

'But…what about Victoria Moss?'

'Victoria who?'. he asked, amusement threading his tone.

She pouted. 'Don't tease…'

'I am involved with her…but only in a business sense. Vicky and I go a long way back…she used to chase after me when I was a teenager. She wasn't my type then…and she certainly isn't now.' His smile melted something deep inside her. 'You're my type.'

She threw him a haughty glance. 'You told me once that you weren't partial to redheads!'

He laughed. 'There's an exception to every rule. You, my love, are that exception.'

Suddenly serious, Whitney said, 'Oh, Luke, if you'd never come back to the valley, you'd never have known that your grandmother had forgiven you for leaving, and that she wanted you to have what is truly your birthright.'

'She must have hoped that one day I *would* come home, and she knew that if I did, I'd remember the secret drawer in her desk, and the letters and love we had once shared. She guessed I'd look for one last letter from her—which is what I did, thank God—and she didn't let me down.'

He took the will from Whitney and dropped it onto the desk. He hauled her into his arms.

'I love you so much!' He kissed her till her head whirled, and then passionately wove his long fingers through the wild tangle of curls framing her face.

'Marry me, my flame-haired beauty—marry me tomorrow!' He grinned down at her wickedly. 'You do love me, don't you?'

'Oh, I love you, with all my heart…more than I'd ever believed possible.'

He engaged her mouth again in a steamy knee-buckling kiss. When finally he let her up for air, Whitney said, breathlessly, 'I do love you, Luke, but…'

A small frown tugged between his brows as her words faltered. 'What is it, my darling?'

She expelled a shaky sigh. 'Have you *really* put the past behind you?'

'Absolutely.'

'But…what if, one day, you start to wonder if you'd been wrong about me?' She couldn't keep the shadow of doubt from her voice. 'What if you wonder if I married you for what you have—the Emerald Valley Vineyards—rather than what you are?'

He was silent for such a long time, she felt her heart quake. *Was* that going to be a problem for him?

And then he smiled. The smile started slowly, at the edges of his lips, and gradually spread till it was wide. Eyes twinkling mischievously, he picked up his grandmother's final testament, and before Whitney could even gasp, he had ripped the thin sheet of paper into a hundred pieces.

'Luke!' She stared aghast at the scraps drifting like snowflakes to the floor. 'You can't do that!'

'I can't?' He scratched his head. 'I thought I just did!'

'But…*why*?'

'I had to put your mind at rest. The only question was, how to do it! My grandmother provided the answer. You know what they say—where there's a will, there's a way.' He put his arms around her and drew her close to his heart.

Whitney gazed up at him, hardly able to take in the huge scale of the trust he'd shown in her. Dizzy with love for this man who had once been her enemy, she whispered, 'So...partners now?'

'Partners forever, my darling.' He kissed her again, tenderly, and his kiss was a promise. 'Forever and a day.'